Gilbert C. and Montana H. R. Walking Bull, 1972

O-HU-KAH-KAN

Poetry, Songs, Legends, and Stories

By American Indians

Gilbert C. Walking Bull, Oglala Sioux
Artist, Singer, and Poet

Montana H. R. Walking Bull, Oklahoma Cherokee
Author and Poet
1913 - 1987

ISBN: 1-57579-322-9

Library of Congress Control Number: 2005909787

First, Second, and Third Printing
by the Iteminzer-Observer Press
Dallas, Oregon 1975

Fourth Printing
by Pine Hill Press
Sioux Falls, South Dakota 2006

Other Books by Gilbert and Montana Walking Bull

WO YA-KA-PI
Telling Stories of the
Past and the Present

MI TA-KU-YE
About My People

E-HA-NI WO-E
In This Powerful Manner
They Expressed Themselves Long Ago

Printed in the United States of America

PINE HILL PRESS
4000 West 57th Street
Sioux Falls, SD 57106

FOREWORD

So often books by and about Lakota elders start with the credentials of the elder and the elder's lineage. My regard for Gilbert Walking Bull comes not from his credentials or his lineage; it comes from my experience of Gilbert. Gilbert holds a vision of a world in harmony, of a people living peacefully together, full of respect and wonder for their environment and all who inhabit that environment (All my relations!).

Gilbert remembers remnants of his people's wisdom, a wisdom forged from countless generations of people living close to the earth and at its mercy. To this he adds his own deep, intuitive understanding of human nature. To sit with Gilbert is to experience the sound advice of a wise elder in the practical aspects of living.

Beyond the advice of the elder, Gilbert penetrates into an unseen world where synchronistic events, prescience, telepathy, and animism that may seem magical or superstitious to the western mind are natural phenomena of a holistic creation unbounded by the limits of technology and a 3-dimensional science. With Gilbert this multi-dimensional reality is expressed as optimism, hope for a better world, and a path to personal empowerment and well being. To experience Gilbert in the sweat lodge is to experience a path to one's physical and emotional healing and re-birth.

Gilbert is helping to revive the ways of his people — their stories and songs, their religion, their traditions, and social norms. More importantly, Gilbert draws upon his heritage to help us all transcend our materialistic mindset and to remember for ourselves how to live healthfully and happily as individuals and a people.

Steve Dudley
Big Horn, Wyoming
2006

Sioux Sacred Pipe, owned by Gilbert C. Walking Bull.
The stem was given to him by his uncle, Lame Deer,
Rosebud Sioux Sacred Man.

Chan-nupa i-hun keya, wan-kan ki,
u-ha, wa-che un-ki yapi na,
u-ha, un-ki chi uz-a pina,
u-ha, za ni-yan un-yan pik-te

We pray, we seek,
We wed by the sacred pipe.

For John (Fire) Lame Deer,
Sacred Man of the Rosebud Sioux,
author of **Lame Deer, Seeker of Visions,**
and relative of Gilbert Walking Bull,

and

The Native American Student Association
Oregon College of Education
Monmouth, Oregon

Presidents
Darlene Folz Peters (1972-73) Klallam
Buzz Night Pipe (1973-74) Rosebud Sioux
Lavonne Lobert (1974-75) Klamath
Duane Azure (1975-76) Santee Sioux

CREDITS

Photography, William F. Wehner, Educational Media Center and staff, Oregon College of Education, Monmouth, Oregon.

Illustrations, Gilbert C. Walking Bull, Monmouth, Oregon. Cover picture is a graphic representation of the original painting, "A Man's Vision" by Gilbert C. Walking Bull, p. 45.

Personal tribute to Richard E. Meyer, folklorist, Professor of Humanities, Oregon College of Education, for his encouragement.

Sioux hand drum, p.1, and the tipi lamp, p. 27, are made by Gilbert C. Walking Bull.

The oil paintings from old Sioux designs are by Gilbert C. Walking Bull and are photographed by William F. Wehner:

> "Sacred Seven" p.10
> "Seven Ritual Colors of the Sioux" p. 16
> "The Power of Life" p. 20
> "Birth" p. 22
> "Power to Grow" p. 35
> "Bish-ko" p. 43
> "A Man's Vision" p. 45
> "The Power of Prayer" p. 48
> "Church at Wonded Knee" p. 54
> "Seal of the Oklahoma Cherokee Nation" p. 55

Appreciation to Donald J. Weiss, Professor of Humanities, Oregon College of Education for final editing.

ACKNOWLEDGMENTS

Some selections in this book have appeared in previous publications, and the authors acknowledge permission to reprint:

Art and Culture of the American Indian, a Guide for Adult Education Leaders (1971), Oregon College of Education, Monmouth, Oregon. Permission granted by editor Montana H. Rickards: Love Song of the Oglalas, and Oglala Sioux.

Anthology of Poetry (1970), Humanities Department, Oregon College of Education, Monmouth, Oregon. Permission granted by editors Donald J. Weiss and Montana H. Rickards: From the Wilderness, Youth, and The Pity of it All.

Singing Birds (1971), Anthology of Poetry from the Humanities Department, Oregon College of Education, Monmouth, Oregon. Permission granted by editors Donald J. Weiss and Montana H. Rickards, Monmouth, Oregon: Out of a Portland Hilton Hotel Window, Hope, Wolf Bird, In Early Morning, The Sickness, and The Loner.

OCE Calapooya Collage of Poetry (1972), Humanities Department, Oregon College of Education, Monmouth, Oregon. Permission granted by editors Donald J. Weiss and Montana H. Rickards: The American Indian, Native Son, Sun Dance, Stuck with the Color Orange, and Death Trap.

Calapooya Collage of Poetry (1973), Humanities Department, Oregon College of Education, Monmouth, Oregon. Permission granted by editors Donald J. Weiss and Montana H. R. Walking Bull: On This Sacred Mother Earth, Old Loyalties, and The Indians Are Coming.

Calapooya Collage of Poetry (1975), Humanities Department, Oregon College of Education, Monmouth, Oregon. Permission granted by editors Donald J. Weiss and Montana H. R. Walking Bull: I Touched You and Sparks Flew, The Witch, Propriety, White Buffalo Calf, Grandmother Spider, The Mortgage Paid, Oath of the Fearless Warriors of the Lakota, Sacred Eagle, The Legend of a Warrior who Turned into a Snake, Stone Boy; and The Mission Bell, the Jaguar and the Wrecked Train.

CONTENTS

AUTHORS

Gilbert Charles Walking Bull

Born in Hot Springs, South Dakota, and a member of the Oglala Sioux at Pine Ridge Reservation, South Dakota, Gilbert Walking Bull is of distinguished Sioux ancestry. He is the son of Edna Weasel, Oglala, and Charles Walking Bull, Rosebud. His father was a student at Carlisle Indian School in Pennsylvania. His grandfather was Move Camp, and his great grandfather was the Prophet Sitting Bull. His maternal grandfather was Henry Weasel and his great uncle of the Oglala band was Crazy Horse. His grandfather, Move Camp, gave him religious training in the traditional Sioux manner. Gilbert attended the Holy Rosary Catholic Mission School and the Lincoln, Nebraska preparatory school. At present he is continuing his education at Oregon College of Education. He is also a poet and artist in residence at Monmouth, Oregon.

Montana H. Rickards Walking Bull

Born in Butte, Montana, and a member of the Oklahoma Cherokee Nation, Montana H. R. Walking Bull is of Cherokee descent on her mother's side. Her mother was an Arkansas Cherokee from Little River County. Her grandfather was Noah Albert Green, whose family was moved from North Carolina to Indian Territory (Arkansas) before 1838. Her father, Benjamin F. Hopkins, was of English descent, and a minister in the Methodist Episcopal Church, South, for thirty years in Oklahoma. Montana grew up in Oklahoma, attended Oklahoma public schools and received her Bachelor of Fine Arts Degree from the University of Oklahoma as well as her master's. She received a doctorate from the University of Oregon and is presently a Professor of Humanities at Oregon College of Education, Monmouth, Oregon. Her two sons, George Guy Rickards and Earl R. Rickards, live in the Portland area.

INTRODUCTION

The poetry, songs, legends, and stories in this issue represent both the oral and the written expression of the American Indian from the great Sioux nation and from the Arkansas Cherokee. They illustrate the diversity of Native American thought.

The first section is the work of Gilbert C. Walking Bull with translated songs of the Sioux people, the legends that were told to him as a child and young person by the elders of both the Rosebud and the Oglala people. He has been working for the past several years in notating and scoring the songs, especially for use with the guitar and principally for his own use as a singer. Since he is bi-lingual, speaking the Teton Sioux dialect (Lakota) and English, he is able perhaps to get a more accurate translation, at least more in keeping with the thought patterns of the people. Some of his poetry in the book is original, and the tales he tells from the reservation are in his own words. These he is able to do through remembering both what he heard first hand and what was told and retold by the people. Gilbert Walking Bull is a full-blooded Sioux and a traditional Sioux in his religious beliefs, and his training in this manner is reflected both in his writing and in his art work, not to mention his musical scoring (offered here in the original as he worked it out himself, not tampered with in any way by a musicologist), and his singing--which has to be heard to be appreciated.

The poetry in the second section especially reflects the Indianness of Montana H. R. Walking Bull. "Sun Dance" was composed on the Rocky Boy Reservation several years ago. "Baking Bread at San Juan Pueblo" was composed in New Mexico. "Wolf Bird," "White Buffalo Calf," Grandmother Spider," as well as some of the others, such as "The Stallion," are her amazing dream poems. "Toltec Image" was written after the poet had read Bierhorst's **Four Masterworks of American Indian Literature** and after she had just finished several days working with Klamath and Modoc Indians in a workshop at Southern Oregon College in 1974.

Mary Ann Cadow Green Hopkins, mother of Montana, contributed much to the writing talents of her children, telling them stories and weaving into them the beliefs of her own people, the Arkansas Cherokee.

GILBERT C. WALKING BULL

Sioux hand drum made and owned by Gilbert C. Walking Bull.

Listen to the Sacred Drums

Listen to the drums
of the great Sioux Nation.
Listen to the drums
of the great Sioux land.
In times of despair,
no one stands alone
when the sacred drums
begin to beat,
when the sacred drums
are heard across the plains.
All tribes will listen
to the sacred drums
of the great Sioux Nation,
and peace, freedom and oneness
will once again
fall upon their hearts
as they become one
with the sacred drums.

1

GILBERT C. WALKING BULL

Oath of the Fearless Warriors of the Lakota
(a translation)

My brother, my friend, my blood,
Generous was he in time of need.
When someone was in need of help, he was there.
Because of his generous ways
No one could say a bad thing about him.
Above all, the greatest respect was given him
Because he took the Oath of the Fearless Warriors
    of the Lakota.
Now when ceremonials are held, they praise him
For his good deeds among the helpless.
Though he has gone to war and has not returned,
His spirit still lives among us,
For he is my brother, my friend, my blood.

GILBERT C. WALKING BULL

On This Sacred Mother Earth

Anywhere, any place,
I live and roam
on this sacred Mother Earth.

Anywhere, any place,
I fearlessly face my foes
on this sacred Mother Earth.

Anywhere, any place,
I count coup and conquer foes
on this sacred Mother Earth.

Anywhere, any place,
like the sacred Eagle my spirit roams
on this sacred Mother Earth

--Translated from the Lakota by Gilbert Walking Bull. Explanation of the song: As a man faces his enemy, he sings the "Indian Brave Song." He sings it also in times of distress.

GILBERT C. WALKING BULL

Rocks Not Happy In Sacks

My dog Gimo knows rocks not happy in sacks.

I met my friend, the rock man, in Redmond.
He was from Indiana, and we talked about thunder eggs.
Next thing I know when I get home,
he sends me a sack of rocks.

These rocks stay in sacks long time,
and I forget I have them
until Gimo tears at the sack.
He knows rocks not happy there.
He growls and pulls at the sack,
and it comes to my mind
that rocks are sacred to my people,
that rocks **are** people and belong to the earth.
So I pick up the sack and look around
for a place for them to rest where they can be seen.

Now rocks are settled and happy on the earth,
not closed up in dark sack anymore.
I put them in the flower bed near the window
where I can look out to see them,
and anyone else can see them getting the sun, the wind,
and the rain. Each day they look happier.

GILBERT C. WALKING BULL

Sacred Eagle

You fly high above all winged ones,
You fly so high that your back touches
   the bottom of the Great Mystery's land.
You soar endlessly across the Great Mystery's
   sacred land,
watching over his sacred people.
When a prayer has been said because one
of the Great Mystery's children
   is in need of strength,
when you soar above, we know our prayers
have been heard and good omen shall come.
Great Mystery taught my people through you,
   and we shall have strength.
Sacred as you are, we proudly wear your feathers
to remind us every day of our lives
to thank the Great Mystery for creating us,
his sacred people, the Lakota, the Sioux.

"Cherokee (Lakota Wiyun)" with words and music by Gil Walking Bull was sent to me by mail on February 22, 1971. It is at the request of Mr. Walking Bull that the lyric and music be notarized as his original production.

Montana Hopkins Rickards

GILBERT C. WALKING BULL

The Birth of Falling Star
(Oglala Legend)

Two maidens fell in love with two stars that were so bright in the sky at night. "I will marry that one," said one of the girls. "I will marry that one," said the other maiden. They laughed softly and looked up at the stars that they had selected as lovers. That night as they slept, their star lovers appeared before them. "We have come to take you away to the star land," they said. One of the stars was young and handsome; the other one was old but still strong and handsome. The younger star chose one of the maidens, and the older star chose the other one. The young women went with their star husbands to their new home in the sky. There they soon settled down with their husbands. Everything was given them that they could want. The young woman married to the older star grew unhappy, for though the old star was rich and could give her anything she wanted, she did not love him.

When the young women went out to dig turnips, they were told they could dig as many turnips as they wished, but there was one root they must not dig. The older star husband went out hunting every day, and one day when he was gone, his wife went out to dig turnips. It was then that she decided to dig up the forbidden root, for she was curious as to why they must not dig it up. She dug and dug and finally pulled the long root out of the ground. To her surprise it made a hole in the sky and she could look down through the hole to see the earth, her real home. How beautiful it was! There were her people down there: her mother, father, sisters and her brothers. How she longed to get back to the earth! Suddenly she made up her mind that she would go back to earth. She shared her secret of the hole in the sky with the other girl. They began to save some deerskin thongs to make a long rope. This they did in secret. When they had what they thought they needed to lower the unhappy wife down to the earth, they pulled out the root, and the unhappy wife slipped down through the hole. She would be leaving her old, jealous husband forever. The other maiden preferred to stay with her young and handsome star husband, but she was willing to assist the other woman by tying one end of the deerskin thong to a tree. Down, down the unhappy wife fell, but the deerskin rope would not reach the earth, and she was held suspended over the earth. She looked down where her people were camping and longed to be with them. She knew she would have to fall without the rope the rest of the way. She was pregnant and wanted her baby to be born on earth, so she began to untie the rope and let go so that she would fall near the camp. She fell to her death. As she hit the earth, her body broke open, and the baby was born upon the earth. The Indians camped below had seen a falling star and hurried to where it fell. They found the dead body of their daughter and the live baby. They buried their daughter and took the baby with them. It was called Falling Star.

"Sacred Seven," by Gilbert C. Walking Bull.

GILBERT C. WALKING BULL

Stone Boy (Oglala legend)

This young maiden was an only child, very beautiful, and she was the pride of her parents. They watched over their daughter very carefully, for they wanted nothing bad to happen to her. One day the girl was out on the hillside picking up pretty rocks when she saw a small, black shiny stone. She picked it up and absentmindedly put it in her mouth and accidentally swallowed it. It was not long after that, that she discovered she was pregnant. She told her parents, and they began to look around for some young man she might have been with, but none was found. She then told them about the small black stone that she had swallowed. When her child was born, it was called Stone Boy.

Stone Boy very early showed that he had extraordinary powers. He lived with his grandmother, and she began to help him make arrows for his bow, so that he would become a great hunter and warrior. People did not honor him as they did the other children as they considered him a bastard child. The first time that Stone Boy took his bow and arrow out, he saw a large buffalo sharpening his horns on the brush. He stopped and spoke to the buffalo.

"Grandfather," he said in the language of the buffalo, "why are you sharpening your horns?"

The buffalo straightened up and answered. "We have heard that if we do not get together as a herd and charge Stone Boy in the spring, he will kill us, for we have heard that he has special powers."

Then the boy said, "I am Stone Boy." He took one of his arrows and killed the buffalo.

On another day Stone Boy saw another Buffalo sharpening his horns on the brush. He said, "Grandfather, why are you sharpening your horns?"

The buffalo answered. "We have heard that Stone Boy will kill us, and we are sharpening our horns so that we may be ready to charge when the clouds come low to the earth in the spring."

Stone Boy told the buffalo who he was and killed the buffalo. It was not long before Stone Boy had asked many buffalo why they were sharpening their horns, and always he received the same answer: they were afraid that Stone Boy would kill them because of his extraordinary powers, and they were getting ready to charge Stone Boy in the spring.

Stone Boy went back to his grandmother and told her that they must make many arrows before the clouds came low to the earth and the strong winds began to blow, for that was the time the buffalo planned to charge and kill Stone Boy. Stone Boy and his grandmother made over two thousand arrows to be ready for the buffalo herd the next spring. About the time Stone Boy thought the buffalo herd would begin their charge, he threw a stone to the ground, and it began to grow. He put his grandmother and his mother and the two

11

thousand arrows on the rock. He climbed up on the rock with his bow, and the rock continued to grow until it became a huge boulder. Then he began to hear the thunder of the buffalo herd. The wind blew hard and the clouds were close to the ground, but he was ready when the buffalo charged the rock. The noise of the buffalo was like thunder as they charged the rock and broke their horns as Stone Boy shot them from his position on top of the rock.

One by one they were dying when Stone Boy heard a voice from the buffalo herd. One of their leaders cried out: "Let us go back or we will all be killed." Those who yet lived turned away as Stone Boy's arrows shot forth. Many of the buffalo lay dead, and the people who saw what had been done by Stone Boy recognized that he had special powers and never called him a bastard again. He became a great leader among his people.

GILBERT C. WALKING BULL

The Great Hunter (an Oglala legend)

There was once a boy who had a great gift. He was to be born in the village with a great gift. He was to be one of the great hunters. So when this child was born, those around him--his playmates, and even his parents, began to notice him--the way he does things. In those days when a child became a certain age, the grandparents gave the child playthings like a lance, bow and arrows, or a knife to practice with. So when this child was born, his grandfather made him a bow and arrows, tomahawk, and knife, and he taught him how to use these things when the boy came of age. When he went hunting, he took these things with him on horseback. When the boy came of age, the old man took the boy hunting with him and taught him how to use the bow and arrows, to hunt certain games, such as animals, small games, and as the years go, he learned to be pretty good, and everyone became aware of him and his ability. They knew before he was born that he would be a great hunter. They knew that this must be the one. Everyone had a great respect for him. When he goes out, he never wastes anything--only hunts what is needed and required in the village. He always brings something home from hunting and always shares, especially with the elders, and they have a great respect for him. He always hunts alone.

So one day he went out hunting, and his parents and people in the village heard about it. They expected him to bring back something. He did not come home that night, so the chief adviser called a meeting to select the greatest trackers to find his trail and track him down. They were afraid that the enemy might kill him, ambush him.

So the trackers follow his trail, pick it up and follow it almost for a full day. When the sun passed midway, the trail came to a dead end. Where this was, a staff was stuck in the ground. So they searched several hundreds of yards near where the staff was stuck to see if he had come upon foul play, but they could find nothing. They returned to the village and reported the news to the chief advisers. So the following day, they selected the greatest warrior-horsemen to search out where he might have been killed by the enemy. They searched in vain and reported they could find nothing. Thereafter, his relations and those that knew him went out to see if they could find a clue that would tell them something about what had happened to him.

One day his family was worrying about him. They felt he was dead, and they were sad. The boy's mother cried. Someone then walked into the tipi. They all looked and here **he** had walked in. The news got around the village. The chiefs and advisers had him come to a designated tipi. They knew something strange had happened to this young man, and they wanted to know about it. In order for him to tell the truth, it was the custom to sit down and smoke the sacred pipe first. After he smoked the pipe, he told his story.

He said the day he went out hunting he went places where he thought he could find game, but there was none. He went over where he thought he could find game on the other side of the mountains. As he was walking at the foot of the mountains, in flat country, where he could see miles off in the distance, while he was here, he heard a swishing noise. It was the air swooshing down upon him, and just as he was going to look up, something grabbed hold of his arms. He reached around, and just as he looked around he saw the greatest claws he had ever seen on the largest eagle he had ever seen. He grabbed hold of the eagle's legs, but the eagle was so powerful, he had no chance to fight it off. The eagle lifted him up as though he was a feather and flew away with him. As they soared higher up in the air, the eagle talked to him and told him not to be afraid because the eagle knew that he was a great hunter and would be coming his way and would be in need of his help.

The eagle said, "Do not be afraid, for I am taking you to the nest." When they landed in the nest, here they found two baby eagles, both huddled in one corner of the nest, both afraid of the newcomer that the mother had brought. She told the babies not to be afraid of the man because he was the one who would protect them. The mother eagle then told her story as to why she had brought him to the nest.

"For so many springs, I have tried to raise a family here, but so many times when they reach the age that you see them now, a certain animal comes and kills them and eats them up. That's why I knew you have certain powers as a great hunter and I brought you up here to kill this animal. I will tell you when this animal comes, and and you will prepare for him. In the meantime I will go out to get meat to bring back so you can eat with my family."

For several days the mother and father eagle bring in an antelope which the hunter makes into jerky meat for himself and to feed to the little eagles. Since he was so high up on the bluff, he saw his people and the trackers trail him but could do nothing. One day getting toward noon, way up high--as far as you can see--were the eagles soaring making screeching noises. The father eagle swooped down coming close to the nest. He said "Be prepared. The animal is coming. He will come from the edge of the cliff, south from where you are sitting."

The baby eagles huddled into the corner of the nest making screeching noises also because they were afraid. Several times the father eagle flew close to the nest saying, "He is getting nearer." So the young hunter knelt down just inside the nest. He took his bow and arrows and aimed toward where the eagle had told him the animal would be. While he sat, out of nowhere a big head--such a big head-- that looked like a bear's head, stuck his head up, but so fast the young hunter could hardly tell what it was, but he knew right away the animal would poke his head up again. The arrow flew through the

14

air and hit the animal right between the eyes just as he stuck his head up a second time. When the arrow hit, the thing straightened up and fell backwards over the cliff. In that instance, high above, the mother and father eagle soared. The mother eagle made the tremolo sound as the elder women make when joyful or happy. At the same time the father eagle sang an honor song as he circled high above. Then pretty soon both landed near the nest and the father eagle said to him: "You have killed the biggest snake that has killed my family for many years. For this reason, from here on, your arrows will be accurate and you will be guided by my people, the eagle people, and your power shall be strong and nothing shall happen to you. Nothing shall be impossible for you as long as you shall live." The eagle gave him feathers to make a war bonnet as he said: "In a few days my son and daughter will take you back where you were found when we brought you here."

The baby eagles were practicing how to fly, soaring up in the air. The day came when the father eagle told him: "Now they are ready to take you back to the place where you were picked up."

The hunter told how he grabbed the legs of the young eagles according to the father eagle's directions and stepped off the cliff. At first, the wings of the young eagles came down. The father eagle pulled them up so they could gain altitude again, and the young hunter was taken back to the place where the eagle had found him. This was his story to the chief and his advisers.

"This is how it happened," he said. "This is how it is."

(This legend was told at Monmouth, Oregon, October 1974, **spoken** by Gilbert Walking Bull. The traditional bilingual Oglala speaker, may use the present and past tenses interchangeably as he speaks in English. This is as the speaker spoke it with no changes instituted. The noun sometimes gets an **s** added in the speaking, such as games in referring to game to be hunted. A tremolo is a high-pitched wavering sound Indian women make when happy. The honor song is tribute paid for one who has earned distinction.)

"Seven Ritual Colors of the Sioux," by Gilbert C. Walking Bull.

GILBERT C. WALKING BULL

The Man Who Turned Into A Snake (Oglala legend)

Two young men who sought to become warriors and belong to the warrior clan went out on a mission to seek out the enemy and to prove themselves worthy. They were gone several days but found no enemy even though they actually were close at one time to the enemy camp.

They were beginning to get tired and were in need of food. Finally they decided to go back to their camp. On the way back they stopped to rest at a cave under an overhanging cliff. Inside the cave they built a fire so that the enemy might not discover their whereabouts. There were some old bones in the cave, and one of the young men began to throw the bones on the fire. Right away something was happening, for the bones turned into good smelling meat.

"Look," said the young man who was throwing the bones on the fire, "the bones are turning into meat." He reached forward to pick up some of the meat, for he was very hungry.

"There is something very strange about this," said the other young man. "I would not eat it."

The other young man kept right on eating the delicious meat. He ate and ate until he was filled and not hungry anymore. They decided to go to bed in the cave, for night had come. They covered themselves with their blankets for a good night's sleep. It was not long after they lay down that the young man who had eaten the meat called out to the other.

"Something is happening to me. Please raise my blanket from my feet and see."

His friend lifted the blanket to look at his feet and found something growing out from his toes. "It looks like the tail of a rattlesnake," he said, "that is growing out from your toes."

"Then we must cut the tail off," said the man who had eaten the meat. His friend took a sharp knife and cut off the snake tail. They both decided they had better leave that place in the cave in a hurry. His friend bound up the wound, and they started back as quickly as possible, but on the way back to their camp, something kept growing out from the toes and up the legs of the young man who had eaten the meat.

Finally he could no longer keep up with his friend and begged to stop. "I can go no further. I will rest for a little while. Please cover me with my blanket."

They rested for awhile and thought they might try to go on. When his friend lifted the blanket, the snake's body had grown up to his waist.

"It's no use," said the affected young man. I cannot go back. I must stay here. Please go back and tell my relatives that I cannot live with them anymore. This is the place where I will live," and he pointed to a hole in the cliff nearby. "Please tell my relatives to

17

bring the sacred banners to me in the fall when the Thunder Beings have gone. I will not be able to show myself in their sight."

His friend watched with great sadness as the young man, being transformed into a snake, began to crawl towards the hole in the cliff. His friend hurried home and told the story to the relatives of the young man who turned into a rattlesnake. They got together the sacred banners and the sacred tobacco for the trip they would take when the Thunder Beings had gone. At last they made the trip to the place where his friend had left him. They looked up the cliff where they saw a large hole. Very soon a huge rattlesnake came from the hole towards them. His friend said to the relatives, "Do not be afraid. It is he, my friend."

The snake coiled near them. They placed the sacred banners around his neck and left the tobacco there. They put their arms around the snake's neck and cried. The rattlesnake told his relatives that they might return if they wished and they must not be afraid, but that he would be in this shape until he died and the hole in the cliff would be his home. He asked them to leave something for him when they came back to visit. And they said goodby while he moved slowly back to his hole.

GILBERT C. WALKING BULL

A Story About A White Crow

When I was a kid grandma told us kids this story about a white crow. Long ago a white crow who has a mysterious power and can speak and understand Lakota language, when the hunters go out to hunt games this white crow would fly ahead of the hunters and scare the game away. The hunters would come home empty handed and would tell their story about the white crow. Because of the white crow, the game was so scarce that the camp was slowly but steadily starving. The chief of the camp put out four horses as a reward for anybody who can catch the white crow. That person might have this chief's beautiful horses. Still the white crow was too smart and wise to be outwitted, and the great hunters tried in vain.

Then one day a sacred man in the camp said to his tun-hun (brother-in-law): "Let us go on top of one of those hills and there I shall turn myself into a buffalo and you shall without mercy kill me and scatter me in a big circle, and there I shall catch the white crow."

His tun-hun (brother-in-law) did as he wished, and it wasn't long afterwards that as the sacred man lay there he saw the white crow circling above him. Pretty soon the crow landed on a limb just out of reach and said in Lakota: "I see it is you, Ca-oo (He's coming), by your doing this and trying to catch me, but I am too smart and wise for you." But the white crow was too hungry and beside his curiosity got the best of him so he flew from the limb and landed so far from one of the scattered remains. Each time he hopped towards it, he would say, "You sure look like Ca-oo (He's coming), you got eyes like him." He finally reached the remains and picked at it. In that instant Ca-oo (He's coming) turned himself into a being and grabbed both legs of the white crow. The white crow immediately began to beg Ca-oo to let him go by saying, "Ca-oo, Ca-oo, please let go of me and I'll never ever again do what I have done to your people. Please, please, let go of me." But Ca-oo (He's coming) brought the white crow back to the camp and that night he built a fire inside of his tipi and put lots of green wood in the fire so it caused lots of smoke. He hung the white crow above it upside down. The white crow was saying, "Ca-oo please; Ca-oo, please; Ca-oo, ple..., Ca-oo, . . ., Caw, Caw, Caw."

The sacred man cut him down when his feathers turned completely black from smoke, and also the crow had completely lost his voice. The only thing he can say is caw, caw, caw. That's when the sacred man turned him lose, and ever since then his descendants, when they see a man, they say, "Caw, caw, caw," and fly away, for they think Ca-oo is coming.

19

"The Power of Life," by Gilbert C. Walking Bull.

GILBERT C. WALKING BULL

A Sioux Love Story

This love story was told to me by my grandmother. She lived to be over ninety years old before she went where everybody goes in the hereafter.

The Oglala Sioux camp was below some high buttes. There lived in this camp a very beautiful Indian girl, and since she was the only child, her parents watched over her very carefully. The only time she went out of their sight was when she walked down to the stream for drinking water. On one of these trips for water, she met a young warrior who was so pleasing to her that she fell in love with him at first sight. Eventually, she told her mother about it, but when her father found out, he objected because he said the youth was too young to be talking to his daughter. How could he take good care of her when he hadn't even distinguished himself in the Warrior Society? He said he would forbid her seeing the youth again.

For a little while both the mother and father watched their daughter very closely, but by accident she met the young man on one of her trips to the stream to get water. She told the youth what her father had said of him. He felt bad because he was just about to get ready to go to her father's tipi to ask for his daughter's hand in marriage. When he heard what she said, he told her that he would be leaving with the first war party that would be going out, and forever his name would be remembered among the tribe.

It was well over a month since the war party had left the village, but every day the young girl waited patiently. One day a scout returned with the news that off in the distance, he had seen a lone runner headed towards the village. The council tipi was prepared for the runner where he could tell the news that he had brought.

When the runner reached the village, they recognized that it was one of the men who had left the village with the war party. He told them his story about how they had encountered the enemy and how they had had a running fight. He told how again and again a young warrior had delayed the enemy while the others had gotten away, and finally the runner was the only one left alive to tell the story. The news spread like a wild fire. Around the encampment the story was heard.

That very evening the people in the encampment heard a girl singing a love song so beautifully on top of the highest butte just west of the camp, and, as everyone looked up, they wondered who this girl could be. They watched in awe as they saw that she had her beautiful buckskin dress on, and as she was singing, she walked backward off that high butte to her death. It was so sad, for she was the only child of her parents and the most beautiful one in the village. She died bravely for a warrior that she had fallen in love with at first sight.

GILBERT C. WALKING BULL

This butte still stands high and mighty just northeast of Fort Robertson, Nebraska (near the present town of Crawford), where my great uncle, Crazy Horse, was killed by a stab in the back from a cowardly, glory-seeking cavalryman.

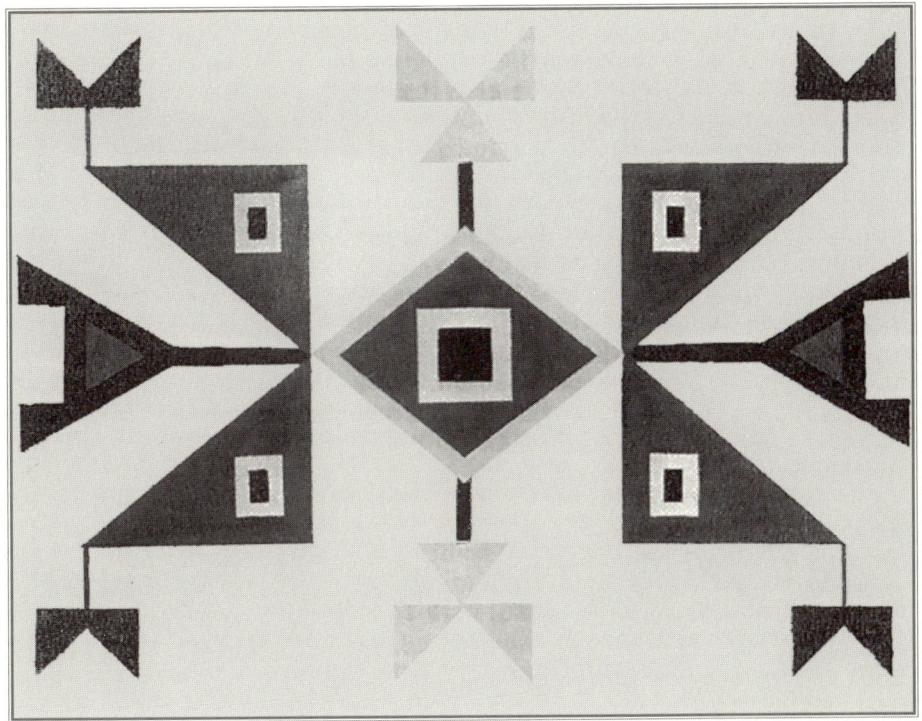

"Birth," by Gilbert C. Walking Bull.

GILBERT C. WALKING BULL

An Old Incident in Sioux Country

I was old enough to remember this incident. I lived with my grandfather, Move Camp, and during the evening time lots of the old warriors who fought in Custer's last battle still lived in those days and came around to grandfather's house. They told stories all evening long. One of these stories I still remember well.

When they first put Indians on the reservations, the old ways were still honored greatly. For example, when someone dies they hold a wake for four days, and at the end of the fourth day, they bury their dead. This is the old ritual for putting away the dead, still honored even today. As this one story goes that one of the old Indians was telling, there was a wake being held and two hungry sisters went mainly just to get fed. (It is also the custom at the wake in the old way to serve food at midnight for those who pay their last respects.)

One of the sisters was so hungry that she paid attention only to the old farm clock which stood across from her upon a shelf. On this night it was awfully windy outside and all the "wakers" were scared to go outside. It was also kind of dark where the coffin was, and everyone at the wake was very quiet. It was along about this time when the hungry sister, still paying attention only to the clock, noticed that the clock had stopped at fifteen minutes to twelve. She got so excited that she spoke out loud, thinking she was speaking only to herself: "Oh, look, it stood." She actually spoke in Sioux the words, "ma i-na-shi ye." You see, "i-na-shi" means both "stop" and "stood." Without a moment's hesitation, the wakers misinterpreted the word. They thought she said that the corpse had stood. Immediately they were stacked up in the doorway trying to get out of there. Windows flew open, and they scattered like a bunch of quail. All this disturbance because of a hungry woman!

(Note: A person can point his finger at a car when it comes to a stop sign and say, "I-na-shi," or "It stopped." Likewise, he can point his finger at a person's getting up out of a chair and say, "I-na-shi," meaning, "He stood up.")

BRIAN

SORRY I MISSED YOU
AGAIN - FOR THE CHECK
HERE'S NATHAN'S BOOK
AND I COLLECTED THE VIDEO

TALK TO YOU SOON

JOHN

GILBERT C. WALKING BULL

My Episcopalian Uncle

One of my mother's uncles was an Episcopalian minister. He preached hell fire in our native tongue, Lakota. His name was Jim Willson, and he was one of the guys from the Pine Ridge Reservation that were sent to Carlisle Indian School in Pennsylvania. He didn't stay very long, but when he came back to the reservation he was converted to this church because he had a little of the white man's education. He asked the tribal council to build him a church because he had just been baptised and that gave him the right to become a minister of that church. Well, the tribal council had a church built for him. You see, back in those days the tribal council still retained the old traditions, so when a man said something in regard to the religion, they would take his word for it. For this reason he became a minister of the Episcopal Church in that district.

During one of my uncle's hell fire sermons he said, "You can't even trust your own wife with a secret unless in the pit you wish to be burned, for like a wolf preying on a small animal the Devil is lurking in hearing shot."

His wife challenged him on his remarks about wives. She said, "Woman can keep a secret until her dying day." Anyway, this family argument or hot discussion went on for quite awhile, and it finally leaked out into the family circuit. Pretty soon others heard about it, and the older people said, "I-Washi-CHU" (loud white man argument).

Then one night at my mother's uncle's place, just as they went to bed and blew out the lamp, they had a couple of dogs that were making all kinds of noise out towards their chicken coop. He got out of bed and looked out the window. He said, "There's something or somebody out there trying to steal the chickens." He rushed over to the clothes closet where he kept his shotgun and shells. He got them out and put on his pants and shoes in the dark in a hurry and rushed out of the house. It wasn't long afterwards that his wife heard a shot. A little while later he came in the house with blood all over his hands, pants, and on his bare chest. He said, "Wi-yan" (Woman), real loud. "A man is trying to steal chickens but when he saw me coming, he took off running so I shoot him dead, and you better help me make a coffin and bury him right away before morning comes or it will be too late."

She was so startled because of what her husband said that he had done, she jumped out of bed, slipped on her dress and shoes and grabbed her blanket. She was ready to get the hell out of there. He stood in the doorway so she couldn't get out. He said to her? "If you figure on leaving, you better do something about the back side of your dress, Wi-yan (woman), or otherwise the dead man might roll over." She looked back and realized that is was the dress she had been making that afternoon. She hadn't finished the back part of the skirt. It was the one she had slipped into in the rush. In those days clothing materials were hard to get for those who lived out in the country, so they saved flour sacks from government issue rations and they made undergarments out of them. So right across her rump on her panties there was NOT TO BE SOLD marking on them.

Her husband told her. "You better move the table and the chairs in the kitchen out of the way so I can make a coffin out of that wagon box." While she moved things out of the way, he went outside and took his one and only wagon he and his wife used to go places in, took it apart and in a hurry made a coffin out of that wagon box right in the middle of the kitchen.

When he had finished he told his wife that he was going to take the coffin out there and put the body in it." When I finish, I'll call you and you can help me carry the coffin out in the middle of our plowed field. We will bury him. In the meantime get that lantern ready."

So while he took the coffin out, she got the lantern ready, and it wasn't long afterwards that she heard him calling her. She went out there and helped him bury the coffin. It was awful heavy, and they had to stop several times, but they finally reached the spot where he wanted it. After they buried the coffin and got back to the house, he told her that it was a white man that had long red whiskers that he had killed. "And I want you to swear on this Holy Book that you won't tell a single person," he said. And so she took the oath and swore that she would never tell.

Things went well for a couple of months until one day as he was riding on horseback from the village he saw a couple of Indian police cars at his place. The sight of the police cars made him think that, being minister to the Almighty, they had come for him because someone had died or had been hurt. He urged his horse to go faster and it galloped on home. Just as he got to the house, the Chief of the Sioux Indian Police was there in person waiting to arrest him. He told my uncle, "for we heard that you killed a white man with long red whiskers and buried him right in the middle of that plowed field." He pointed his fingers right towards where he buried that paleface. "And we want you to take us over there and we'll dig him up."

So my mother's uncle reluctantly got off his horse and took them over where the grave was, and it seemed as though from out of nowhere all of a sudden lots of people were showing up. They all gathered around the grave site while the Chief of Police and his deputies were digging out the grave.

Jim Willson (the minister) stood quietly, but all this time he kept his ears open and listened to the crowd to see if he could tell how they happened to know all about this terrible incident. He overheard one of his leading disciples say, "Why, it's a shame and a disgrace for such a man who had us believing that he was a chosen man to lead us to Him," and he pointed his fingers toward heaven. "Why, he shot not once but several times and then he made his wife bury this big white man with red whiskers. He shall burn in hell, that's for sure!" This disciple of his made it sound as though he was there when the incident took place.

And others, they said, had heard the story straight from the horse's mouth. Well, the police finally dug up the coffin, and the Indian Chief of Police ordered the others to get out of there while he jumped down into the grave with a crowbar held in his hand. He started in on the coffin trying to pry it open while the whole crowd gathered around the grave like bees on their bee hives. The appointed one of the Indian police that was supposed to watch Jim Willson (the minister) was just like the crowd. He was so excited to see the white man with long red whiskers that he forgot to watch Jim, so Jim edged around the crowd where he could see their expressions when this man with a star opened the coffin. When Jim turned and looked around, it just dawned on him all of a sudden that the whole reservation had come to see this terrible incident and the murder he was supposed to have committed. There were Model T's, wagons, people on horseback and on foot as far as he could see, and people were still coming. Meanwhile, back in the hole, the sweat was pouring out of the Chief's forehead while he was frantically trying to pry open the box. Knowing that this was going to take place, Jim, the minister, had put lots of nails on the coffin. When the Indian Police Chief finally got it open, that white man with the long red whiskers he expected to find was a big red adult male domestic fowl (big red rooster, that is), and also there were a couple of sacks of sand to weigh down the coffin with.

When the tension broke, things finally settled down from the laughter and the embarrassment amongst the crowd for their being taken in by a big false rumor. Someone noticed it when he looked over the coffin again that all the excitement of wanting to see the white man with long red whiskers caused them not to even notice that the coffin was only three feet long.

Jim, the minister, told the crowd to listen to what he had to say. He said, "Brothers of the Police Force, I know you all mean well, and I thank you for it, and also to those who like to see that justice is served well. I am asking the police to rebury my one and only rooster who gave his one and only life to prove that you cannot trust your wives nor can you be taken in by false rumor. Today is an awful nice day for you all to come to visit my place, and to those of you who came a long way to see me in person and to see what I look like, I thank you in person, for it is well of Wa-kan Tan-ka (the Great Spirit) that we have gathered under him with one heart. Ho-he che-tu we-lo (So, it is, indeed!)."

Painted tipi lamp with Sioux motif, by Gilbert Walking Bull.

At My Grandfather's Place

At my grandfather's place during the evening time, right after supper, the men would move to the south side of the room, while the women who came with their husbands for the evening would help grandma wash the dishes. Afterwards they would gather on the north side of the room. It is in my people's tradition to socialize in this manner, for there are times when one is in need of the confidence of his fellow man, or for woman's talk in regard to personal problems.

Among such a group there is always one with great wisdom, and he or she has the right to give advice. For those who hear one's personal problems, they have no right to ridicule nor to criticize. Those who break the unwritten law are thereafter marked as untrustworthy until such time as they may have their own problems and may need to seek advice from any one of the known advisers. That is when they get reprimanded, and this usually straightens them out and others that are marked as untrustworthy for the rest of their lives. We Sioux call them Wo-yah-kehs-ah (Ones who cannot mind their lot).

My grandfather, Move Camp, was a great holy man amongst our people, the Sioux. He was well known for his doctorings throughout the country amongst the Indian people, and they came from as far away as New York, Florida, Canada, Texas, California and Washington. He never turned anybody away, as far as I can remember. Before he passed away, there were as many as twenty tents or more pitched around his place at a given time. Usually they came from the surrounding reservations like Standing Rock, North Dakota; Cheyenne River, Lower Brule, Yankton and Rosebud from South Dakota. They camped for two or three weeks at a time. One thing I liked about it was that all the time I met some of my blood relations whom I never knew existed.

The old warriors are the ones that gathered at grandpa's place practically every night, and they would tell many stories of the past and what was happening at the present time as well as what was going to happen in the future.

The very word Wa-shi-i-ju in my beautiful Sioux language means, "One who stole the tallow." Long ago, a story has it that one of the scouts that was posted in one of the four cardinal points of the village relayed a message that from the east a lone rider was approaching the area. You see, my people, the Sioux, long ago, when they moved camp or were camping, had their scouts assigned. The village chief and his seven advisers carefully chose these scouts, and they were sent out a distance of about four miles. There were also scouts located about two miles out and then there were scouts who watched over the horse herds. So, in our Sioux oral history which I was taught when I was a kid by some of the old people who were still living then, they had never mentioned anything about the Sioux village that was surprised in an attack by cavalrymen. My great uncle Crazy Horse's village was attacked because he thought he could trust some of his men. He had sent them out as scouts, but they turned out to be turncoats. The chief sent out several warriors to bring in this invader so they went out, and it wasn't long until they brought in a white man who looked more like a bear than anything else because his face was covered with hair. Those who had never seen a white man thought that it was that i-ya (the giant).

There was a sacred man in the village who could speak all languages fluently, but he was gone at this time to another village, so the people put the white man in a tipi. They wanted to feed him something to eat, but they didn't know whether he would eat jerky or pemmican or not, so they left him alone. The white man was hungry, but he didn't know how to communicate with them. There was a real old lady living with her granddaughter in the next tipi over who had lots of tallows hanging from her jerky rack, so the white man would look around and when he thought that no one was watching him, he would slowly sneak on over to where the tallows were hanging, and he would slip a piece of it under his coat. He would sneak back inside the tipi and wolf it down. Back in those days tipis were made of hides and it was hard to see anyone's shadow from the inside or from the outside, so they had a "deadly warrior" stationed right in back of the tipi watching the white man through a peep hole. Thereafter for a time they would call the white folks they came in contact with "wa-shi-i-ju (tallow stealers)," or at that time "One who steals tallow from that old woman, (Heh wah-shi ah man-u)."

GILBERT C. WALKING BULL

Indian Cowboy

During the horse and buggy days on the reservation when someone held a dance, regardless of how far away it was, men and women would go to it on horseback. One time my great Uncle Charlie Red Breath Bear and a couple of his friends went to such a dance, but on the way he said that his horse went lame. It was at night, and the moon was not shining, so it was awfully dark. Right alongside the wagon road he saw some horses grazing. He said he got his old lariat out and roped the biggest one. He said it was very wild and the meanest he had ever put a saddle on. He would rear up and paw the air, but he said he finally broke him of that and rode him to the dance. He tied him to the hitching rail where all other horses were tied. He said, "Grandson, in those days we danced until break of day." He said he danced all night, and when it was getting towards daybreak all kinds of commotion was happening outside. Horses broke their reins, and those outside sparking their girls ran about frantically. He said he looked out towards where he had about tied his horse, and here a grizzly bear was tied to the hitching rail with his saddle on him.

My great uncle Charlie Red Breath Bear went where all good dogies go, but his humorous stories are still with me.

Then again, one day when he was rounding up his strays, he was too busy to pay any attention to the weather, and all of a sudden a bad hail storm sneaked up on him. About fifty yards ahead of him hail as big as his fist bounced all around him. The only thing he could do was turn his horse around and make a bee line for home — about five miles in the direction the storm was moving. He had a race with the hail storm. He just let Old Paint have his rein, and the old horse threw both of his ears back while hail was bouncing up right behind him, and he could reach out to catch it if he wanted to, and just as he dashed into the barn, the hail hit like a machine gun. He said, "When I unsaddled Old Paint, that's when I first noticed that all the hair on his tail had been knocked off. There was nothing left but the raw tail, and it looked just like a piece of leather hanging back there."

GILBERT C. WALKING BULL

A Prophecy

On an evening a story was told about a Sacred Man who could speak all languages fluently, and he made others to speak and understand the English language.

Ku-te I-yankapi (Shooting Chasing Him) was one of my grandfather's cousins, and they say that when he was young he fasted up on one of those sacred Paha Sapa (Black Hills of South Dakota). He stood for four days and four nights. He told his story that on the third morning just before the day broke from the east he saw across the sky the covered wagons that were heading towards where the sun goes down, and behind the covered wagons the machine age was coming: cars were followed by trains and air planes and jets, and following the jets the atom bomb exploded, and a little before the sun rose, right above him a flock of seagulls were circling. They were making noises and something told him to listen to them very closely, so he did. Somehow he began to understand them. They were talking English. Pretty soon they all changed to speak other languages. At last, just as the sun's rays shot across the sky, on them he saw rider after rider on horseback pulling travois, and behind them women and children were walking.

They said he interpreted his vision this way: Wa-kan Tan-ka (Great Spirit) has revealed a great vision to me that from the east a strange race will come and they will invent many things out of your Mother Earth and out of your Father's breath, and in doing so, they will destroy themselves and anger Wa-kan Tanka (Great Spirit). He gave me the power to speak all languages and to teach my people so they may protect themselves from this strange race. I have also seen, that like the power of the sun rays, the Indian Nations will rise. This vision has been given me by Wa-kan Tan-ka (Great Spirit). Ho-he che-tu we-lo (So it is indeed)! In the village they say he organized a school, taught hand-picked scouts and the Fox and Strongheart Societies to speak English, French, and German and in one language, Sioux, to speak to anyone in any race, and they would understand, and, in turn, they can speak to him in their language and he would understand them.

GILBERT C. WALKING BULL

A True Story of a Runaway From Genoa Indian School

When the first reservations were established, many of the Indian children were sent to far off government schools, such as Carlisle in Pennsylvania; the Genoa, Nebraska school, the one at Rapid City, South Dakota; Wak-paLa School, South Dakota, and others. From the Pine Ridge Reservation one of my great uncles, Chan-te T-in-za (Brave Heart Man) was in his teens when he and several others were sent to Genoa, Nebraska. Even so, he would rather be wild and free and retain the old ways if he could have chosen. So it was that not long after they took him there he ran away heading back to the Pine Ridge Reservation. In those days truant officers were very mean, and when they caught up with a runaway, they would horsewhip him. In trying to catch a runaway, the officers would ride horses, and sometimes they would run over the runaway to try to make an example of him. My uncle said that the truant officers were white men, but they didn't have much education, yet they were trying to educate someone. He said, "The only education they have is bitterness, and I've got a lot of that too."

In telling his story, he said: "I left during the night through a window, and I knew that they would be tracking me down by using the older boys from different reservations--the Omahas and Winnebagos. They were our enemies at one time, and they still have the old feeling. They help the washi-i-ju-wi-tko-tko-kas (psychopathic white men), tracking lots of runaways, until they find them and they stand by watching while the wash-i-ju-wi-tko-tko-kas (psychopathic tallow stealers) whip a brave Sioux, and I believe this is the only way this to-kas (enemies) try to get even with the Lakotas (Sioux). But since I have a father who belongs to the Fox Society, he taught me the ways of a fox, to be smart and cunning and pretty sly. I outfoxed them when they picked up my tracks the next day. I knew that they would be catching up to me the next day, so during the night I built a small fire by the creek. I made my footprints leading towards the creek, only towards where the water is coming, and I crossed over and made my tracks towards where the water runs. Then I got into the water and came back upstream for quite a long way. When daybreak came and when it was light enough to where I could make things out clearly, I got out of the water like any fox would do, sneaky-like, and I kept to where the high grass is so that the to-kas (enemies) would not come back and pick up my tracks when they found out that they had been tricked by an old Fox Soldier's son.

"All that day I kept to the high ground, and every once in awhile when I came up on a higher hill I would lie down and look back towards where I had just been, but so far I could see no one following my trail or whatever there was that I left to be seen. I believed that the old Fox Soldier's trick had done the trick. Of course, those to-kas (enemies) are real easy to trick when someone has the instinct of a fox like me. Ho-he che-tu we-lo! (So it is indeed) About the second day I crossed the Pan-keh-ska Wak-pa (North Platte River), and I followed it for awhile and then I headed Wa-zi-ya taki-ya (Northwest). About the fourth day when I came across some Yankton Sioux, they were awful nice to me. They gave me something to eat and a place to stay for the night. Before I left the next morning, they gave me some pa-pa-sa-ka (dried up meat or jerky) and they warned me not to show myself when I came upon any settlements because people in them are told to turn in any young Indian they see alone in the hills and they would receive pay for it by the school I had just come from. They showed me which trail to take. I walked and sometimes I trotted long distances at a time, and when it got towards evening time I came upon an old wagon road. Here I was sort of undecided which road to take, so I sat down and ate what little of the pa-pa-sa-ka (dried meat or jerky) I had left while I decided which way to go.''

He continued, ''It was in the ptan-yetu (getting towards fall), and it gets cold when it gets dark, so I finally decided to take the old wagon road because it looked as though it sort of cut across towards where I was heading. It was a full moon that night, and it helped me find my direction. I walked and trotted and walked again, and finally when the moon was west of me I came upon a small hill. When I got to the very top of it, I could see things off in the distance. I saw smoke coming out of a log house. Something told me to go there and warm up.

''This old wagon trail I had been following since the sun had gone down bypassed a road that ran in front of the log house. When I got close to the house, I could make out that it was only one room with a small shack attached to it. I also noticed that there was someone standing outside a little away from the house. When I got pretty close to him, he said, 'Hau kola!' (Hello, friend). I said, 'Hau' (hello), and then when I got right up to him I could see that he was an old man. His hair was so white it looked like snow on his head. His hair hung to his waist, and he had a cane in one hand. He said, 'Every since Ni tuka-shila mahiyaye he han-tan (your grandfather went down to the west, or the sun went down) I knew you were coming this way, so I warmed the place up and waited for you.' He said, 'Come right in.' He went in, and I followed him. I noticed when I went in that the floor of the shack was a dirt floor and upon the shelf above a small table there was a lantern. Next to the table there was a stove, and next to it there was a single springs bed.

''The old man said, 'I know, you've been traveling a long way for the last three days, but tomorrow when your grandfather passes the center of the earth (noonday), you shall see your relations. Your father and I long ago counted many coups. We both belong to the Fox

Society. We don't know the meaning of running away from the to-kas (enemies). Grandson, sleep there on that bed and sleep well, for tomorrow shall be a great day for you.' He turned and walked into the other room. I was so tired, and the warm air made it all the worse. I didn't even ask his name. I just lay down on the bed and went right to sleep. During the night I rolled over on my side and opened my eyes to see whether daylight had come yet, and I noticed the old man was smoking his peace pipe, for I could see the glow of the light in his pipe bowl. I fell back to sleep, but somehow I felt that the old man had gone outside and had come back in because of the sound of the closing door.

"The coldness kind of woke me up, so I opened my eyes just a little bit to see, and here it was daybreak already. I didn't look around; I just closed my eyes and tried to go back to sleep, but it was getting colder, and I didn't hear the old man moving around. I couldn't go back to sleep because the bed I was lying on all of a sudden felt as though there was nothing underneath me. I lay back, and I opened my eyes. Here it was daylight where I could see everything. I noticed that I could see the daylight through the ceiling. I could also see cobwebs hanging all over it. I sat right up and noticed the bed I was lying on had nothing on it but the springs. There was no bedding. I stood up and looked around very carefully, but there was no sign of life anyplace. I walked over to the other room where I had seen the old man smoking his pipe, but there was nothing there but one old spring bed. Since I am a Fox Soldier's son, my heart is very strong, and I understood this old man's helping hand. He knew that I, Chan-te T-in-za (Brave Heart Man) had chosen my Indian ways and would be coming through his place with a heavy heart. From the other side he gave me a place to lay my head. Ho he che-tu we-lo (So it is indeed)!

"Just like the old man had said, I came back to my people about noon, and they were all glad to see me, and I was glad too. During the evening my father and some of the old fellows were sitting around talking after supper, so I told them what had happened to me early that morning. Without any hesitation one of the old men said, 'Why, that's mi su (my cousin), Charging Enemies. He's been gone for over twenty years.' "

GILBERT C. WALKING BULL

"Power to Grow," by Gilbert Walking Bull.

GILBERT C. WALKING BULL

Buffalo That Become Loco

Grandson, those buffaloes you see there in that fence where white men keep them used to be a very powerful herd at one time, and just like the Lakotas the spirit shall come back to them, and they will be great herds again.

Long ago buffaloes used to fast just like the Lakotas. They stand in one spot and they bow to the four cardinal points sunwise. They eat or drink nothing for days, and when they feel the unseen power from Wa-kan Tan-ka (Great Spirit) they become Ta-tanka kna-ski-yan (buffalo that become loco). Their sense of smell and their eyesight become so keen that they can smell a human being a long distance away, and when they are this way, nothing is safe in their sight. A fast runner or a fast hunting horse is not safe nor fast enough when one of these Ta-tanka kna-ski-yan (buffalo that become loco) is in the vicinity. They charge up on a camp, or many times when a Sioux comes across one of them, these buffalo howl something like a Suk-ma ni-tu (wild dog or timber wolf), and they grunt at the same time as they run. So it is best when one hears this sound if he is in a tree area to find the biggest tree and get up in it or get in the nearest hole he sees if it is big enough to get into especially if he is out in the open prairies. Or he might try to lure the buffalo off in the open prairies. Or he might try to lure the buffalo off a cliff if he is in the mountains because Ta-tanka kna-ski-yan (buffalo that become loco) is so loco that nothing will stop him but death.

One of your great aunts, Wa-na-ki Wi (Spirit Woman), when she was young and pretty, married a man who was from one of the Seven Council Fires of the Lakotas (the mighty Sioux). She was not happy with the way he treated her so she left that camp and headed back to the camp where her parents were. In those days, grandson, across the great mountains and plains the mighty Seven Council Fires of the Lakotas (Sioux) dwelt. It was getting towards evening on the second sun when your aunt came to the top of a hill. She sat down to rest when she noticed that off in the distance a Suk-ma ni-tu (wild dog or timber wolf) was sitting very close to her den paying attention to something a distance away. Your aunt looked in that direction too and here she saw what Suk-ma ni-tu was paying attention to. It was a Ta-tanka kna-ski-yan (buffalo that become loco) circling the herd and charging the bushes. All of a sudden Ta-tanka kna-ski-yan lifted his head and sniffed the air and all of a sudden charged towards her. There was no place where she could hole up except in the den of that Suk-ma ni-tu (wild dog or timber wolf). The wolf looked her way then turned and went back into her den, so she followed the wolf in. The den was kind of small so she got her knife out and enlarged the den as she was going down inside it, but that time the Ta-tanka (buffalo) hit the hole awfully hard with his head and tried to dig into it with his hooves, but she kept right on enlarging the hole with her knife as she was going down. Finally she reached the bottom of the den and there the den was pretty wide. She found Suk-ma ni-tu's (wild dog or timber wolf's) two babies, all huddled up in one end of the den. She was very tired from working so hard enlarging the hole that no sooner than she had reached the bottom of the den than she just closed her eyes to rest. She was so tired that she fell asleep. The next thing she heard was someone talking to her. "There's no danger any-more, for he is gone now. Stay, and in time you shall be taken back to your people. There is a weed next to you. Take it and recognize it, for it shall protect you from danger when such things come your way. When such a time comes, break a piece of this weed and stick it in your hair. Sit down and you shall not be seen by the enemy." When she opened her eyes, she couldn't see anything because it was so dark down in there. She fell asleep again. Pretty soon she heard someone say, "Woman, wake up. Your grandfather has given you another day to appreciate and thank him." She opened her eyes and saw the daylight through the hole. She crawled out of the hole and here she found outside a freshly killed antelope which had been dragged back by the male Suk-ma ni-tu (wild dog or timberwolf). She skinned the antelope and made jerky. She cut up chunks of the meat for the little ones. She stayed there for several days.

Just before daybreak one morning she heard someone talking to her. "Wi-yan (woman), from this time on when our people ho pi han-tun (send forth their voice, or there is howling), you shall understand them and do as we tell you and no harm shall come to you. Now it is time for you to go. Your people have moved their camp, and they are south of here. One of us will guide you there." So when she came out of the hole it was just getting daybreak, and right outside there sat a big Suk-ma ni-tu (wild dog or timber wolf), and he said, "Ho i-ya yo (Let us go)." He went, and she followed him all that morning. They traveled south, and every once in awhile he stopped and said, "Ho, a -sni-kiya yo (Rest your strength)." When the sun was in the middle of the earth, he stopped and said, "Paha he el ohk-la-te wi-cho-te ye-lo (Below the hill which we are facing is the camp)." He turned to go. She watched him until he disappeared into the wilderness. She went on towards the hill, and on her way she saw a couple of riders coming towards her galloping. She wasn't too sure whether or not they were Lakotas, and she didn't want to take any chances, so she broke off a piece of the wa-na-ki peh-shi (ghost weed) and stuck it in her hair and sat down. It wasn't long until the two riders rode up, and she heard one of them say. "I swear I saw her come right to this spot." He spoke in Lakota, and she knew right away that they were her people. One of them got off his horse and walked pretty close to where she was sitting so she said as she removed the wa-na-ki peh-shi (ghost weed) from her hair, "I am sitting right here." He really jumped as though he had stepped on a rattlesnake.

They took her back to her people and she told her story to a sacred man, just the way it happened. He said that she would become a great woman as she grew older. And as she grew older, she became as it had been predicted. During the evening or night when timber wolves or coyotes howl, she would go outside alone to listen to them and come back in to tell what they were saying. She was given the gift to understand them. Many times when bad winters came and game was so scarce that hunger fell upon the camp, she would listen to the howlings of the Suk-ma ni-tus (wild dog or timber wolves) and would tell the hunters exactly which direction to go find game. Or sometimes she would tell the warriors that their to-kas (enemies) were near.

Your great aunt, Spirit Woman, lived to be a hundred years old before she left us. Ho, he che-tu we-lo (So it has been told)!

GILBERT C. WALKING BULL

Fulfilling a Wish From the Other World

When they first established the Pine Ridge Reservation, several families from my great uncle Crazy Horse's band chose to move to the northwest corner of the reservation right along the Cheyenne River, which is called in Sioux, Wak-pa Wash-teh (good river). This was so that they would be away from the washi-i-ju-ki (tallow stealers or white men). The men who chose this area were the men who fought along side of my great uncle Crazy Horse when they massacred General Custer. There was Red Shirt, High Eagle, Drags the Rope, Rocky Mountain Sheep, Hollow Horn, Fills the Pipe, Iron Teeth, and Poor Buffalo. All of these families were scattered out all along the Cheyenne River.

Red Shirt and High Eagle lived at the south end of a long table top so that the other districts (the people in them) used to say, og-leh-sha paha a-kan-ti heh (where Red Shirt lived on top of that table top), but eventually they called it the Red Shirt's Table, and when they built the village right along the Cheyenne River, it was called Red Shirt's Table. Just west of where Red Shirt lived and about two miles beyond was High Eagle's place. The road comes in between the places of these two families, running from the south upon this table top and going several miles to the north and moving on down into the Cheyenne River, crossing the river, and on over to the white man's side.

The village was built where the road came down from the table top and down into the river. It was during this time when they were building the village that High Eagle's nephew got a job working at the village and moved his family nearby along the Cheyenne River. Of course, lots of the men who worked there pitched their tents and had their families move there. So one evening High Eagle walked all the way from the table top to the village to visit his nephew and some of his relations. From his place about three miles there was an old school house and from there the road divided into a Y with the left hand road going at the edge of the table top. About two miles further it bypassed a real old long log house, and the family that had lived there had passed away long ago. There was nothing left but the old house. From this place the road led to the edge of the table top for a couple of miles alongside it. Further north it dropped down into the village, and the other road from the school led also to the east edge of the table top for a couple of miles until it came to a graveyard and then to the Episcopal Church. Right next to it was the Catholic Church and its graveyard, and then the road angled off from there to the left where it led to the other road which went down into the village.

It was in the Moon When Cherries Are Ripe (September, and the cherries were Choke), so it gets dark early and it gets cold when the

39

sun goes down. While old man High Eagle was visiting his relations, his nephew asked him to stay for the night, but High Eagle had left his wife alone at their place and she was up in the ages too, and there was no one there to help her in case anything happened to her. He told his nephew that he was going back even though it was getting late in the night. His nephew's wife wrapped up some Indian bread and some meat and put the food in a bag for him to take back to his wife.

When old High Eagle left there, he said it was about midnight. When he came up to the Y up on the table top he was undecided as to which road to take, and he thought to himself that if he took the right hand road it led past that old house, and when someone was alone and came through this way on horseback or when walking at night on the road towards this old house, he would see the light they talked about so much. Then he thought to himself that if he took the other road it led past those churches and their graveyards, and this particular night it was dark and windy, and he felt he had enough troubles of his own in **this** world and had no intention to see someone from the other world. He decided to go in between the two churches and the old house, for there was a trail that went through there though it was seldom used and there were a lot of prairie dog holes in the area and cactus, too.

High Eagle spoke these words at my grandfather's place on the Oglala Sioux Reservation in the 1930's:

"I wanted to get back home, so I started walking. My eyes were getting accustomed to the darkness so I wasn't worried. The only thing that might worry me was wild animals about, but other than that, I was much more concerned in getting back to the house. I walked as fast as I could, then all of a sudden to the left of me towards where the church was I saw something black coming my way. It looked like it was floating. I stopped to see whether it would cross my path and go on about its way, but it stopped and stood there in my path. Right away I knew this thing was not of this world. I sat down, took my sacred pipe out, and I put tobacco in the bowl. Just as I finished filling the bowl, I lit it and offered it to the four cardinal points. This thing that stood in front of me came towards me. When it was closer I saw that it was a man, but he was not of this world. He was tall, dressed in black, and even though it was dark I could see his face, for it was white. He came and stood in front of me. I said: 'Long ago my people have all gone, and I, Wanblee Wan-ka-ti ya (High Eagle) once was a great warrior. Now I am up in ages, and it won't be long now until I will be meeting them. I am a poor man. I have nothing to give. What is it that caused you to stand in my path?'

"This man who was not of this world sat down in front of me, crossed his legs so that I could offer the sacred pipe to him. He took it and smoked it, but I didn't see any smoke coming out of his mouth or

GILBERT C. WALKING BULL

nose. I could see that he took drags of the pipe because I could see the glow in the pipe bowl.

"After we finished smoking the sacred pipe, he said, 'Wanblee Wan-ka-ti ya (High Eagle), the light that they see all the time in that log house -- it is I whom they see. When someone has come my way alone, I have wanted to talk to him, but when he sees my light, he gets scared and goes around me. Today, I knew you would be coming back this way. I know your heart is strong and fears you have not; so, in your path I stand seeking your help, Wanblee Wan-ka-ti ya (High Eagle).' So I said, 'Whatever you wish of me I shall do, Ko-la (my friend). ' He replied, 'Ha-oo (So it shall be)!' Then he said, 'Tomorrow morning go to that house and dig under that north window and there you will find Wo-pun (parfleche). Inside it you will find some money. Take this money and make a big feast. Burn incense cedar and pray for me so that I may get released from this earthly bondage and go to join the others where they are. When I was on your side of the world I treasured the earthly things, and I forgot Wa-kan Tan-ka (Great Spirit). Now my spirit is bound to that money. When my wish is made real the light shall never be seen in that house again, and travelers shall never again have to change their path when they travel through there at night. Ho he che-tu we-lo (So it has been said)!'

"I said, 'Tun-yun eh-he-lo (You have spoken indeed)!' When he got up and left, I watched him very closely, and I could see that he was not walking. He was floating towards the graveyard real fast. After he disappeared, I got up and continued my journey home. It was getting towards daybreak when I got home, but I was not sleepy at all because of talking to the wa-na-ki (ghost). It wasn't long after I got home that some relatives of ours came by. Since they had a car, I asked my grandson to take me to that old log house the same morning.

"When we got there, my grandson said that he had heard so much about the light that they could see in this place that he preferred to stay in the car. It was not that he was afraid, he said, but it was just that he might see something he didn't want to see that might cause him to leave without the car in his haste to be gone, and besides he thought that since there were only two of us, we would need someone to look after the car. He asked me to go ahead.

"I went around with my shovel and dug where I was told to dig. When I got about three or four feet down, I found the Wo-pun (parfleche), and inside it I found the money the Wa-na-ki (ghost) had spoken of. It was all wrapped up in a buckskin. Also there were two beautiful pairs of moccasins and man's vest all done in porcupine quill. When my grandson got through counting the money, I believe he said it was over kok-tun toh-pa (four thousand). I did according to the Wa-na-ki's wishes, and to this day one can travel through there and nothing shall be seen at night. Wa-na-ki (ghost) has gone to the other world. Through this incident Wa-kan Tan-ka (Great Spirit) has taught us a great lesson. It is I, Wanblee Wan-ka-ti ya (High Eagle) that has seen, heard, and done. Ho he che-tu we-lo (So it has been told!"

This story was told to us one evening at my grandfather Henry Weasel's place when I was a kid by old man High Eagle himself, and although he has gone many, many moons ago, his story has stuck with me all these years, and it pleases me greatly to share it with you.

GILBERT C. WALKING BULL

When You See A Rainbow

When the world first resettled, the Great Spirit took some spirits and turned them into human beings and put them on this continent. He called them Lakotas. He took one of the men high up on a cliff overlooking the village down below in a beautiful valley and said to him: "The nation which is camping below I have given you to rule over. Be gentle and kind. The colors of the flowers I have placed with you and your nation, and they shall glow as you and your nation walk through the generations. It shall be a sign others shall see and know that I have placed a great nation upon this continent." He made a sweeping motion towards the beautiful colors of the flowers that grew alongside the cliffs as though he had gathered them up with his right arm. He threw the flowers towards the sky and formed a beautiful rainbow up in the sky. Think of the Lakota Nation when you see a RAINBOW.

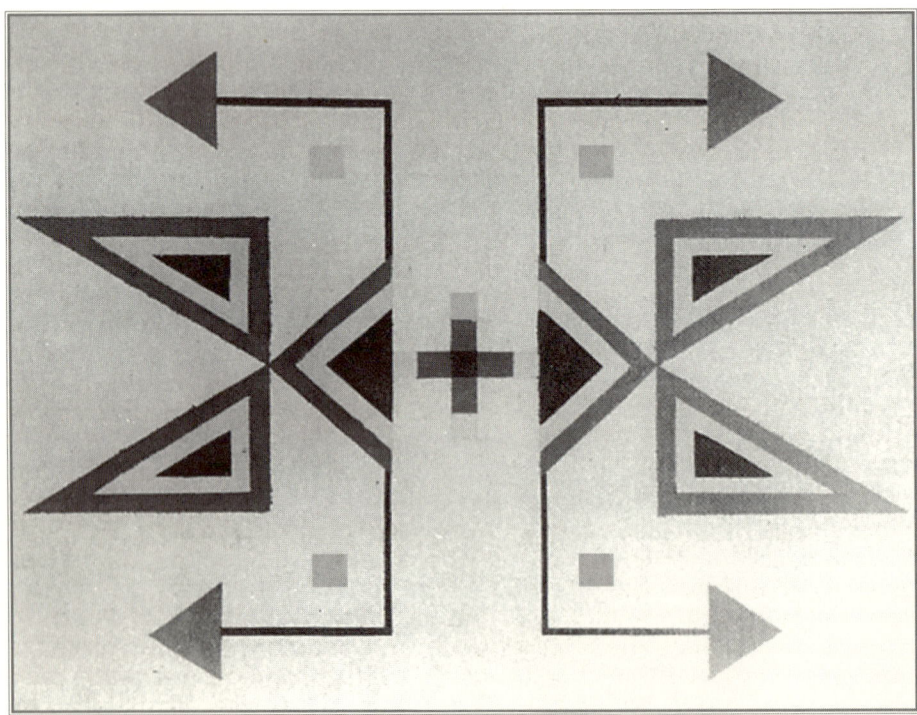

"Bish-ko," by Gilbert C. Walking Bull.

GILBERT C. WALKING BULL

The Fearless Ones

There is a small sand hill located near a small settlement called the Wakpa Mini Lake on my reservation at Pine Ridge, South Dakota. Long before the covered wagon days, when my people traveled through this part of the country, those in need of arrowheads would go to this particular sand hill and there they would find small and large arrowheads, very beautiful ones, and in turn they would leave some Indian tobacco to thank Unkche-kilah (fearless ones) for making these beautiful arrowheads and leaving them for them to use.

Legend has it that long ago there used to be a man-like animal that lived that made these arrowheads, and he used to fight the Thunder Beings. In turn the Thunder Beings fought them with lightning. My people call them Unkche-kilah (fearless ones). They said that they look like something between a human being and an animal, and they live on the slope of a hill. Their weapon looks somewhat like a rifle, and they shoot so accurately that at any given distance they can place an arrowhead right on the mark every time.

They, these Unkche-kilahs (fearless ones), hide under a cottonwood tree or a cliff, and they fight the Thunder Beings during thunder storms, and that is the reason why those who still believe in the old ways used to tell us when we were kids not to go under any cottonwood trees during a storm because every so often the Thunder Beings strike this tree. I was told that one of my great grandfathers saw one of these Unkche-kilahs (fearless ones) just before dawn while he was out with a war party. They had bedded down for the night and when it was getting towards daybreak all of a sudden he heard a peculiar noise coming from someplace. He woke the others up and told them to listen, and they heard it too. They sneaked up on it and here it was one of these Unkche-kilahs (fearless ones) who was target practicing. His aim was deadly. Just before the sun rose, he disappeared. They went to where he had been and found lots of arrowheads in piles. They say that these Unkche-kilahs (fearless ones) live here on this earth like any other human beings too, but they have mysterious power to appear and disappear.

There are countless arrowheads scattered all over the midwestern area. Of course, there are other locations for them too, but there's one particular area in those Grand Teton Mountains of Wyoming where I heard so many stories about my people when they were free to roam. They say that there one could find some arrowheads made out of hard stone instead of flint stone. Once we rode into these mountains on horseback, I and a couple of my blood brothers. I told them about the story and the arrowheads of stones, and it wasn't long afterwards that we found several of them by accident. The smallest one was one half inch long, and the larger one was two and a half inches long. We let them lay where we had found them.

Unkche-kilahs had a weapon that shoots these arrowheads like a modern weapon of today. They say that amongst my people there are persons who have the instinct of these Unkche-kilahs (fearless ones), and that they become great warriors, hunters and leaders. Everything they do, they do accurately. They say that one out of four thousand persons is born with this instinct.

"A Man's Vision," by Gilbert C. Walking Bull.

A Sioux Among the Missionaries

When Indians were first put on the reservations, the missionaries came among my people, and they converted quite a few families. From then on these families would hold a Bible study meeting practically every week in one of the homes. In those days religion was an important part of one's life, and when the white man brought in his religion, it played an important part in the daily life on the reservation too. It was a great honor to have the head of the family hold a Bible study meeting for his oldest daughter or son.

In those days the Government didn't build any meeting houses, so whoever put up the meeting would have to provide the place, so for this one meeting the father and mother bought a huge tent. They pitched it close to the house, and they had their oldest daughter invite all her friends and others too who were interested in joining in with the Bible study.

When the time came that evening, many young people gathered for Bible study. Inside the tent there were tanned hide rugs spread out so all the Biblebacks could sit on them. One young Indian man went there, but he was so bashful that he didn't go inside. Instead, he stood outside next to a wagon full of hay where those who came by horseback tied their horses. He was standing between two saddle horses to keep warm, but still he was cold even though he was wearing a sheepskin coat, for it was December. As time went on, it was getting awfully cold out there. About that time two Indians rode up and tied their horses to the wagon. One of them said to the bashful Indian, "How-kola (Hello, my friend). Do you care to have a drink with us?" He pulled out a quart of wine and passed it around. When it got to the bashful Indian, he thought to himself that he might as well drink as much as he could, for he thought it was the only bottle they had. He really guzzled it down. It didn't take long to finish the bottle, and he thought that was the end of it until one of the guys said to the other, "You might as well bring out the other one." So he unbuckled his saddle bag and pulled out another jug and passed it around. Each time it came around to the bashful Indian, he drank it down like there would be no tomorrow. They finished that one off in no time and here the other guy went to his saddle bag and brought out another one and they finished that one in no time also.

Because it was so cold, the bashful Indian felt as though he was only drinking water, but about that time the father of the girl who was honored came out of the tent. He went to the woodpile to get an armful of wood. On his way back to the tent he looked towards the guys and said "Why don't you guys go inside, for it is awful cold for you to be standing out here. Besides I am sure you came to join the group inside."

GILBERT C. WALKING BULL

One of the guys said, "Ho-ee ya yo (Well, let us go)." The bashful one went in first, but he was so bashful, he pulled down his cowboy hat so low in front that one could hardly see his eyes. He also turned up the sheepskin coat collar and knelt down on one knee behind the heating stove. He didn't feel the heat because he was too cold to feel anything. He knelt there on one knee and listened to what was happening. He began to be thawed out by the heat from the stove. He felt the wine beginning to work on him. He wanted to get out of there, but other people came in and blocked the doorway. He couldn't get out. About that time the Bible was being passed from hand to hand and each person that touched it had to make a brief testimony as to what the Bible meant to him. The bashful Indian sure wanted to get away before making a testimony, but the passing of the Bible was getting so close and he was getting uptight from drinking all that wine. To top it off, he was too bashful to excuse himself and walk out.

About that time the person next to him punched him with his elbow and handed him the Bible. That instant everything seemed to explode inside him: the heat, the wine, his bashfulness. He pushed his cowboy hat back and stood up as though he was one innocent child of God. As he began to make his testimony, he thought of all the things he wanted to say but couldn't because he was too bashful. It all came out because of the false courage he received from the wine. He said: "My brothers and sisters, long ago across the big waters the people over there put thorns upon Jesus Christ's head and they tore his clothes and they spat upon him and they mocked him and they whipped him like an animal, but none of you sons of bitches were there to help him in his despair."

He doubled up his fists and he knocked the stovepipe completely off the heating stove, and the smoke from the stove was like a fog inside the tent. The innocent fellowship scattered like a bunch of quail in all directions, and those who didn't have sense enough to leave in gentle haste nearly suffocated. This, my friends, was an actual happening on the reservation.

"The Power of Prayer," by Gilbert C. Walking Bull.

GILBERT C. WALKING BULL

The Stranger Who Turned Into A Jackrabbit

A bunch of us young warriors went to a pow wow which was held at our district community center dance hall, called pay-yahb-yah (in the middle ones), and as the dance progressed there were lots of real good singers. They sang some beautiful songs, but some of the men folks didn't seem to want to go inside. Instead they all hung around outside looking in. No one but the women folks seemed to be dancing. The men who were inside just sat and watched. My friend and I were standing next to a bunch of older fellows who were bunched up in front of a window looking in on the dance. We overheard their conversation. They were scheming together and talking about beating up on someone when he came out. We edged closer to see what was happening, and we saw the guy they were talking about. He was tall and handsome. We couldn't see his face because he was wearing a big cowboy hat, and I saw the reason why these guys were planning to beat him up. Every time they sang a rabbit dance song, he would pick out a woman and dance with her. He never danced with the same woman twice. We knew then that these guys were going to beat this guy up because he was dancing with their wives and their girl friends.

The word got around among the men outside and those who heard it gathered around just to see a big fight when the dance was over. Well, it was getting close to midnight and some of the families had left early. From where we stood, we could see what was going on inside. I happened to look in about that time, and this stranger, who had caused all the commotion outside because he danced with the women, all of a sudden while he was dancing with a girl, he broke away from her when they danced by the door, and he came out. He caught everybody by surprise and just as I turned to my buddy and said, "He came out!" this handsome dancer came by us. He went in between the two cars back of us. Just as he was right in between the two cars, a little distance away someone turned on the car lights, and in that instant the car lights hit the stranger. A mysterious thing happened right in front of our eyes. It was not only the two of us that saw it, but there were others who saw it too. **This stranger turned into a jackrabbit!** Since some of those who saw this thing happen are superstitious, someone hollered in the crowd, "Catch that rabbit and kill it, or it will bring a curse upon us!"

The rabbit ran right in front of some cars that had already turned on their headlights, and they chased after it. My buddy and I had come to the dance on horseback, so we got on our horses and joined in the chase.

In those days when there was a dance going on in some district, my people came by wagon, horseback, car and on foot. Usually a family's dogs came along with those who came by wagon, and so on this particular night several dogs were in the crowd. Right away they caught on that something was happening. They too joined in the chase. Into the open prairie, down into the dry bed creek and up into the hills and back into the open prairie we chased: dogs, those on horseback, and those on foot. Just before daybreak those on foot formed a line: men, women, and kids. By yelling messages the chase was turned around and everyone headed towards this line. We boxed in the rabbit, and again right before our eyes a mysterious thing happened. **The rabbit vanished!**

Middle-aged people and young people who participated in the chase didn't take it too seriously. They laughed about the things that happened to them during the great chase, but the older ones surely did take it seriously because they said that the Great Spirit had given us a sign and for us to be careful about going to a dance. We all gathered around in bunches here and there, and it seemed that no one could come up with an explanation.

Finally my buddy and I rode on back home, and when we got home grandma set up the table for us to eat. While we were eating, grandpa came in and sat at the table with us. We told him what had happened that early morning, and since he is a great sacred man among my people, he listened until we got through. Then he told us the reason why this strange thing happened. He said: ''Long ago, two scouts were lying on top of a hill overlooking the valley below just before daybreak, when all of a sudden they heard a strange noise some distance away from them. They sneaked up to it and there behind the bushes were some rabbits, two by two in a big circle. In the center there were several of them sitting up and making noises as though they were singing, and others who were in the circle were hopping around them, so one of the hunters said, Let's not disturb them, but let us go back and tell the people about this strange thing that we have seen.' They hastily came back to the village and told about what they had seen out in the hills to their chief. He, in turn, consulted a sacred man. The holy man told them that it was a dance that the Great spirit had revealed to them through this animal, and that they should perform this dance. He said that this dance would bring about understanding among them and would unite the villagers and others who danced it, so they performed such a dance. From that time forth, they called it Ma-sti ja-la Wa-chipi (Dance of the Rabbits).

''Whoever attended a dance was supposed to participate in the rabbit dance for the sake of socialization, but the men folks forgot about this or were ashamed of their heritage and didn't dance the rabbit dance.''

My grandfather said that was the reason why the man had appeared and changed into a jackrabbit -- to remind them of their social dance and how it was supposed to be danced.

GILBERT C. WALKING BULL

This strange thing really happened, and the telling of it explains the origin of the Sioux Rabbit Dance, a social dance, now popular on the reservation or wherever the Sioux people dance.

GILBERT C. WALKING BULL

Thanks, Buddy, For Stealing My Beaded Vest

It is the tradition of my people that when someone in the family dies, and he is highly thought of, the parents give away the most valuable thing that the deceased person has possessed to that person's closest friend. This might be livestock, a saddle, some harness, clothing, or some other thing, and it is up to one's friend to accept the gift. There is one case I know about where the best friend didn't receive anything.

The story has it that these two fellows grew up together just like brothers. One of them had tuberculosis, and it finally got to where he couldn't talk at all. He had to whisper, but his faithful buddy stood by until he died.

Just at the turn of the century tradition still played an important part in the affairs of our tribe, so when this guy passed away, his family held a four-day wake, and at the end of the fourth day he was buried, but his parents didn't give anything to his buddy. He was pretty sad-hearted about it. After his buddy was buried, he rode to the top of a lone hill and got off his horse. He sat down under the shade of a pine tree and thought about how his buddy's parents had treated him. He wondered if he should go and dig up his buddy from the grave and take the valuable things that he owned that were buried with him, just for keepsakes. In those days the most personal things might be a beaded vest, moccasins, rings, watches and money. These were buried with the person. So, the more he thought about the idea of digging up his buddy to take the valuable things they had buried with him, the more the idea became clearer in his mind. He decided he should do it.

That afternoon he rode home, got a shovel and went back to the graveyard. He dug into his buddy's grave, and when he reached the coffin, he took his time opening it. As he was doing this, he was talking to his friend as though he were still alive. He said, "Mi-su (my brother), we have as kids roamed and endured many hardships together, but always we survived. This time you chose to go before me, so while you have left me behind, I would like to keep these things to remember you by. Your parents did not give me anything of your belongings. That's why I am doing this." He reached out to set his buddy's body up so he could take the beaded vest off him, and as he was doing so, the dead body threw its arms around his neck, and that was the last thing he remembered.

When he came to, he was lying right in the middle of the floor of his buddy's parents' place, and someone was pouring water on his face. Along about that time the "dead" buddy stood in the doorway, and he both scared and surprised the hell out of the mourners.

GILBERT C. WALKING BULL

The "dead" buddy told his story when concerned people got hold of themselves after the shock of seeing a dead man come to life. He said that all of a sudden he heard someone knocking at the door (he thought), so when he opened his eyes, he found himself inside a coffin, and the sound he had heard was the pounding of the nails into the coffin, nailing him in forever. He tried in vain to make some kind of noise so they would hear him. He couldn't holler because he had lost his voice from the tuberculosis. He could hear the wailing of his relatives outside the coffin, and the next thing he felt was the coffin's being carried, and its being lowered down in the ground with the dirt hitting the coffin.

He said that he knew that no one but God could spare his life, so he prayed with all his might. He didn't remember how long he prayed, but the next thing he heard was a sound like a scraping, and it made him pray all the harder because he thought that some kind of animal was digging in to eat him up. But by that time he recognized his partner's voice talking to him as he was opening the coffin. He pretended to be really dead, but he opened his eyes just enough to see his partner. When his partner bent down over him to set him up, that's when he threw his arms around his partner's neck just to surprise him so he would know that he was alive.

His partner spun around with him on his back and cleared the pit with the blink of an eye. He was so strong and moved so fast that his buddy was shaken loose even though he tried to hold on with all his might. He ran behind him and yelled at him to stop, but his partner picked up a little extra speed and cleared the six foot fence which was around the graveyard without any effort at all. Down below the graveyard there was a creek wide enough to cause anyone who wanted to cross it to have to wade across. He also cleared this creek without any effort. He ran so fast that when he got to his buddy's parents' house, he had run around the house twice before he burst in.

While the parents of the "dead" son sat inside the house with sad hearts, all of a sudden they heard someone say as he ran past the door, "He's alive! He's alive." Each time he passed the door he said, "He's alive!" So the old man went to the door to open it just as the young man burst in saying, "He's alive!" and then he passed out.

After all the excitement was over, and he finally got hold of himself, he told them that the last thing he remembered was when he had reached for his buddy's shoulders to set him up to take his beaded vest off, and his buddy had thrown his arms around his neck.

He was given many valuable things for saving his buddy from being buried alive, and when his friend died the second time, several years later, his parents made sure that their son was really dead before he was buried.

This is a real story from the reservation.

"Church at Wounded Knee," by Gilbert C. Walking Bull.

MONTANA H. R. WALKING BULL

"Seal of the Oklahoma Cherokee Nation," by Gilbert Walking Bull.

The Stallion

In the distance the shadowy figure
Of a stallion reared and stomped,
        full of fire and strength.
Across from where I stood,
Several Indians were idling their time away
In a fenced field while their horses grazed.
One saddled filly had caught the eye
        of the great stallion beyond.
He left his enclosure, leaped over the fence,
And, as he circled round to meet the filly,
He changed into a handsome Indian,
The tallest I had ever seen.
        He was ready to ride.
He casually and gracefully mounted
The beautiful saddled filly,
And rode away as though she belonged to him.
The other Indians watched him ride away.
His back was perfection--the way he rode that horse
        It was strength,
        It was power,
        It was beauty.
I was in my house
Standing at the door
When the big Indian rode up into the yard.
He said, "Are you having a pow wow tonight?
If so, I will officiate."
His eyes were black coals,
He was so great, so tall,
So utterly a man.
I said, "Yes."

MONTANA H. R. WALKING BULL

Bluebirds and Love

I was driving to work on the old road
taking the winding curves with caution,
thinking again of two people I hated.

Because the hatred grew with my thinking
and the zigzagging on the country road,
I asked myself why I hated them so.

It came to me with such suddenness
that the hatred had once been love.
If so, how then could I hate them so?

I paused to face the question.
Was it because I loved them still?
That was it. I loved them still.

Two fluttering bluebirds appeared in mid air,
graceful on the wing, poised there for view
They were those two, their spirit made flesh.

Instant recognition of the power of thought,
the beauty of love and the strangeness of living,
transcendence in the miracle of bluebirds.

MONTANA H. R. WALKING BULL

American Indian Education Conference 1972

Hundreds of Indians milling, looking, waiting,
   laughing, finding their way about the
   Olympic Hotel in Seattle.

A young, talented, powerful Cree gives the
   keynote address. He explains the new
   federal culture program in Canada.

A girl with feathers tied to her long black hair
   meets the second morning with friends to discuss
   strategy for the day when "Indians take over."

Head bands are prominent--all kinds, some beaded,
   set against jet black long straight hair or
   braids of younger ones.

A Canadian Indian lady explains a program at a
   university where the director of the program
   himself has been in the country only three years.

General greetings continue throughout the second day;
   old friends touch hands and laugh together over
   nothing except old remembrances and being together.

Menominees meet to raise money for their cause;
   they sell banners and buttons alerting all
   Indians to their cause; the Wisconsin group.

The last day there's a general flurry--getting a ride
   with friends to the airport, shaking hands, being
   tired, still laughing, and suddenly the hotel empties.

MONTANA H. R. WALKING BULL

The Day the Indians Stood Up

It was a supervisor's meeting
Attended by college and public school administrators
And supervisors at Oregon College of Education.

The college leader said, "And now let me present
To you an Indian from Oklahoma, a Cherokee, Hee, Hee,"
He nearly collapsed with laughter.

A few solemn faces remained silent, and, to the amazement
Of all there, one by one the Indians stood up.
A principal announced his name and his tribe. "I am Siletz."

An English department chairman announced her tribe, Yakima.
A counselor announced his tribe, Umatilla.
A reading consultant announced her tribe, Lummi.

A school superintendent announced his tribe, Mohawk.
An elementary school supervisor announced his tribe,
Potawatomi. An art teacher said, I am Chippewa-Cree.

A physical education supervisor announced his tribe, Sioux.
And so it went. Twenty of the fifty had Indian blood:
Cherokee, Siletz, Yakima, Umatilla, Lummi, Mohawk,
Potawatomi, Sioux, Tuscarora, Shoshone, Nez Perce, Pima,
Apache, Stockbridge-Munsee, Yurok, Hupa, Coos, Chinook,
Ute, and Warm Springs. And as each spoke, he stood up and
remained standing.

It was the day the Indians stood up.
There was no more laughter; there were no more "hee hees."
The Indians had invaded the education sanctuary, and

IT WOULD NEVER BE THE SAME AGAIN.

MONTANA H. R. WALKING BULL

Bird of Heaven (a song)

There in the blue, blue heavens
I see a flash of fire,
Come to me, bird of heaven,
Come to me, heart's desire.

Winged in your flight to glory
Winged in your bright red glow
Send me your message gladly
Let me be sad no more.

Low in my earthly bondage
Seeking to know my fate,
Send me your message gladly
Let me no longer wait.

Redbird, you do bring gladness
You give me hope once more
Redbird, forgive my passion,
Oh, just to hold you close.

Now that you see me standing
Eyes to the heavens blue,
Oh, Redbird, please come near me,
Say you will grace my door.

There in the blue, blue heavens
I see a flash of fire,
Come to me, bird of heaven,
Come to me, heart's desire.

MONTANA H. R. WALKING BULL

The Call of the Indian

To know an American Indian is, or can be, an awful thing.
The Indian will possess you, get inside your being
And roam around. He will take you over completely.
He will go into your being to see what the house
Inside you is like.

I have withstood this kind of possession all my life,
And it isn't easy. First, there was my mother, who
Would have possessed me if she could, and she really tried!
She was subtle and wise and crafty and persistent;
She was so winning with her warm love.

Something in me always said, "No, mama, you can't have me.
You won't possess my soul or my mind; they belong to me."
Momentarily she would give up, but soon she was back with
New strategy. She was Indian. Once possessed by an Indian,
The merger is most demanding, for possession means servitude.

I have seen lives ruined with such love. So, beware of
The call of the Indian -- the sweetest, most loving
Call in the world.

MONTANA H. R. WALKING BULL

Father and Son

I reached out to touch his hand,
his big hand.

The baby nestled in his arms,
happy.

I said, "What do you think
of your son?"

He didn't say anything, just looked
at the baby

So cozy in his arms, its nose turned up.
Then he looked at me.

That's all there was to it.

MONTANA H. R. WALKING BULL

The Corn's About Ripe in Huron (a song)

Oh, the corn's about ripe in Huron
And the sunflower's turned to the sun;
The corn's about ripe in Huron
And the great Missouri flows on.

The face of the Sioux in Huron
Too majestic for me to describe;
The corn's about ripe in Huron,
And the great Missouri flows on.

MONTANA H. R. WALKING BULL

At the Depot

It was depression time,
And I was at the State University
Starving.
My parents were moving
From Yeager to Wheatland
In Oklahoma.
They would change trains
In Norman.
They asked me to meet them
At the depot.

There wasn't much time,
But I saw them:
Papa, mama, and my brothers
And sisters.
Mama told me about it
After papa died.
Papa had said that day, "It was so hard . . .
She reached out her little brown hand,
And I had so little to give her."

I don't remember my special need,
Nor what the money was for,
But today, the thing that sticks
In my mind
Was papa and mama at the depot
In Norman.
Papa, always so courteous,
And mama by his side,
And the briefness of it all--
The love that was there that day
At the depot.

MONTANA H. R. WALKING BULL

Sun Dance

In the still Northern Montana evening,
Beyond small rolling hills, lies the Indian camp,
A circle of white dots in the verdant valley.
Peaceful and expansive below the Big Bear Paws
Is the scene of the sacred rites of the Sun Dance.

Inside a temple made of choice timbers,
Banked and hugged by green foliage from the forest,
Giving privacy to singers, chanters, drummers and whistlers,
Are the tired eyes of those who fast, those who pray that
   the creator will protect the people,
   there will be peace and harmony among all men,
   the youth will be saved from war's ravage,
   the sick will be cured,
   the tribe will prosper.

Prayer cloths hang from timbers for special needs.
At last, the final moment comes when elders hold the
Cloths of red, purple, green, blue, orange and yellow
Which billow from the center pole
And with eyes lifted and with hands pressed upon the folds,
 bless all within the temple and beyond the temple.

Aged grandmothers, eyes closed, fervently press hands
Against the central pole and make prayers amidst tears.
Slowly, each member lays a hand against the pole in
   supplication.
Following the time of prayer, the Chippewa-Cree leave,
And the temple lies bare of singers, chanters, drummers
   and whistlers.

White visitors enter to take pictures of the sanctuary,
Sensing the uneasy distaste of their departing red brothers.
The empty outdoor temple will stand with its cloth entwined
About the central pole until Time brings deterioration.
The temple will become one of many that stand in silhouette
Against the tranquil beauty of the Northern Montana sky.

Next year there will be another Sun Dance, a new temple,
And new prayers to be said for Rocky Boy's and Little Bear's
Chippewa and Cree, who for many years were the homeless,
The dispossessed, the courageous, until their pleas
   were heard

And a home was found on the lands of deserted old
                 Fort Assiniboin.

Here they rear their families in peace,
Here they graze their cattle on the lush grasses,
Here they range their ponies in the hills
That rise in eternal beauty over the valley of the
                 Sun Dance.

MONTANA H. R. WALKING BULL

Wolf Bird

Wolf head and bird tail,
She stands in the center
of the whirling disc.

She goes round and round,
Wolf ears listening,
feathered tail swirling.

Thus she commands the animals,
beasts of all degree, size,
shape, and color.

But none gets near
the whirling disc
where wolf bird stands
and swirls her feathered tail.

At a motion the beasts
will move to the rhythm
of the swirling feathered tail,
the august fanlike bird tail.

In vain you will lock and bar
your doors and secure your windows.
The animals will enter;
the assault will come
at the signal of the feathered tail.

MONTANA H. R. WALKING BULL

The Indians are Coming

The Indians are coming: warriors in front,
  riding furiously, horses in sweat,
  feathers flying.

The Indians are coming: all of them,
  coming right down the road,
  twentieth century style.

The Indians are coming: red skin glistening,
  coming down the paved highway,
  whooping and crying, arms flying.

The Indians are coming: tipis following,
  four rows in file, coming, coming,
  whitely shining, neatly pointed.

The Indians are coming: men, women, children,
  filling the four-lane highway,
  filling the living space, advancing.

The Indians are coming: all in order,
  warriors in front, dust flying,
  voices crying, legs flying.

The Indians are coming!

MONTANA H. R. WALKING BULL

Old Loyalties

Rising up in aloof splendor,
  a tipi stands in front of an unpainted
  small frame building
  in the heart of a busy city
  where the steady beat of ancient drums
  issues from the board walls.

Rising up in ancient splendor
  remote in the densely-crowded city
  stands the tipi surrounded by
  children who play and romp
  as their elders beat their drums
  and sing their ancient songs.

Rising up in a fine white majesty,
  stands the tipi, its use pronounced
  as a dressing room for dancers
  who "feather up" as they drink
  from a battle someone has whisked
  inside from a battered truck.

Rising up to offer protection,
  the tipi holds her own--
  the young men who laugh with
  the bottle as young children
  lift the edges of the tipi to see
  what's going on in there.

Rising up to tell its story,
  the ancient tipi's aloofness
  from all but the romping children
  and the young men to shield,
  the ancient drums beat steadily
  as young women mildly scold.

Rising up, its peak eternally visible,
  the ancient tipi's meant to hold
  its strong young men steadily drinking
  from a bottle to hold them fast and close.
  Women beseech them to stop drinking
  but old loyalties still prevail.

MONTANA H. R. WALKING BULL

The American Indian

A rock, a stone, a tree.
He stands motionless
Unhearing, unresponsive, inviolate.
Speak not to the rock
Speak not to the stone
Speak not to the tree.

He stands motionless
Unhearing, unresponsive, inviolate.
There is more to tell of him;
Surely there is more to tell
Speak not to the stone.

MONTANA H. R. WALKING BULL

Unseen Hands Upon the Clippers

Dull shears snap at the dead gladiola stems
while the sun shines hot upon my head.
I pile the dry stems upon the dead grass
and push on to finish the bed.
It is noon, and the time is short,
For I have to get back to work.
Suddenly, the shears begin to snap
and crack. The handle moves
without my power, though my hands
are still upon the wood.
Under a considerable power
the shears move across the
gladiola bed on their own
as though they were automated.
I am simply the amazed spectator.

What unseen powerful hands
grasp those handles
and cut those stems?

Finally, deciding I cannot
believe this thing that is happening,
I lift the clippers to examine
the bolt that holds the blades together.
Surely there is some logical explanation.
At the moment of examination, the power stops,
and I return to clipping
with the dull shears.

MONTANA H. R. WALKING BULL

I Remember Oklahoma City

A city of shimmering heat in summer,
Snow, ice, and bitter winds of winter;
Black oil derricks against the yellow
   glow of evening.
Chugging rotaries and pumps;
Roughnecks, tool chasers, pumpers,
All of the slow drawl, friendly, but tough!
A city with a river of sand and slums nearby;
Schools separate for white and black;
City boastful of its state capitol building
And its outspoken but shrewd governors
And hard hitting, hard driving senators;
A city of big buildings and residential palaces
And tin can houses of depression days
And packing town with its trailing odors:
A city sitting on the red land of red men
Who gave it its name: Oklahoma City!

Our People

Black eyes
Black, braided hair
Glowing red skin
Beautiful straight backs
Warm loving ways
Sacred ceremonial dances
Mystic, inscrutable thoughts
Proud, expressive speech
Visionary dreams
Native Americans

MONTANA H. R. WALKING BULL

You Gave Me Your Hand and You Smiled

You were sitting on the ground
  with two or three other Indians.
You got to your feet and held out your hand,
  and I took it as you smiled at me.
It had been so long since we were together.
  You were an Indian again as I had known you.

"We have five or six things to do," you said,
  "and we want you with us."
I nodded my head that it would be all right;
  you smiled and sat on the earth again.

Toltec Image

Green-eyed Toltec with tongue of fire,
Four-lipped red man with laurel leaf bar.
  Your green cupped earrings
  Are circled emerald stars.
With your neck thrust forward, gold adorned,
What is your message, god from afar?

MONTANA H. R. WALKING BULL

Baking Bread at the San Juan Pueblo

I.
Our mission was to visit the Pueblos of San Juan, Sandia, San Ildefonso, Santa Clara, San Felipe, Laguna, Acoma, Santa Domingo, Taos, Picaris, and others, half of the nineteen, and we could not do this without our two Indian friends, Geronima Montoya, head of a crafts school, and her assistant, Garcia Marcelino, a weaver and artist, both of the San Juan Pueblo and the Ike Oweenge Crafts Coop. We visited the Pueblos through the generosity of the Governors of those Pueblos. Each Governor shook our hands and bade us enjoy our stay. Such friendly, warm people of the Pueblos! We saw the San Felipe Corn Dance, a ceremony of fertility, a thing of beauty! We participated in the feast day at the home of one of Geronima's friends. We visited the ruins of the Sandias and of San Juan where we had permission to pick up some old pot sherds. We went down into the kivas at Picaris, and we saw the foot race at Taos Pueblo. We ate breakfast with the people of Taos, and we saw the uranium mines at Laguna. We saw the beautiful pottery at San Ildefonso, and Acoma was out there in the desert alone beside the Enchanted Mesa.

II.
We were told we could help with baking bread at San Juan, so on Wednesday night we mixed the dough with the ladies who assembled at eight o'clock at the Talachi home. There were about fifteen, young and old. Three large pans were placed on the dining room table. The elder women were selected to mix the dough and assembled at their places at the table, ready for the dough mixing ritual. Others stood by holding ingredients: white flour, whole wheat flour locally grown and ground, vegetable shortening and margarine, the yeast cakes, warm water, and other necessary ingredients. They might have been surgeons at an operating table receiving aid from a covey of nurses, the way the ladies of the San Juan Pueblo stood by, ready to assist in the pouring of the flour from the sack, ready with the salt while the great bread makers of the Pueblo mixed the dough to the right consistency. There was no measuring cup, no measuring spoon. The palm of the hand served as cup and spoon. Bread boards were laid out next by the ladies, and ritualistically, everything was carefully organized. The younger women kneaded the dough, two ladies to each pan of dough, each kneading the dough until the elder ladies, standing by, pronounced that it was ready to be placed in the pans to rise during the night, and all would meet the next morning for the baking in the outdoor adobe ovens.

MONTANA H. R. WALKING BULL

III.
We were now ready for the baking of the bread. Each of the three pans was uncovered and small amounts of the risen dough were placed on small bread boards for kneading. Thirty-six small bread pans appeared as if by magic. And, as each small ball of dough was kneaded to the inspection of the older ladies, it was put onto the small aluminum foil pans. In the meantime, outside, the oven of adobe was in preparation to receive the bread. A fire of twigs had been made before the pans of dough were kneaded and made ready for the small pans. After the burning of the wood in the oven, one of the ladies swept it out. **This lady was the keeper of the fire**. She swept the oven out and mopped it out with a rag dipped in water from a bucket nearby. After the oven was cleaned and inspected by two of the older women who were seated under the shade of a tree, the bread in the small pans was brought outside for baking. This too was ritual. The bread was brought to the oven in relays, each lady bearing several pans of the dough. As each was brought, the lady at the oven door received each and skillfully placed each pan in its proper place in the oven as others watched to make sure it was done according to accepted tradition and ritual. At last the pans of dough were ready which had been allowed to rise a second time. In the meantime the ladies made the pies and cookies, for one does not waste a hot oven. When all was in the oven, the opening to the oven was closed shut with a board propped shut with a rock. The bread, as it baked, was watched over carefully by the oven tender and the ladies who sat under the tree to advise. If the oven seemed too hot, it was cooled by placing a wet cloth over the entrance.

IV.
While the dough was rising in the house and while the oven was being prepared for the baking, the San Juan ladies cleaned up after the bread making and went into quick action to make pies and cookies. Again ritual ordained certain duties for certain ladies, according to the lady's age, honor, and distinction. The pie and cookie dough was mixed by the elders. These ladies also stood by to instruct the younger ones in the baking ritual of the San Juan people. Dried prunes, which had been soaked the night before, were strained and the juice from the straining saved. The seed was removed, and the prunes were mashed by one of the older ladies. Another stood by to pour in the juice as instructed by the lady who stirred the prunes. In the meantime, some of the younger women were rolling the pie dough to fit the flat tin, and the dough was rolled paper thin, fitted to the flat tin, and the prunes were spooned in to cover the dough, but not too thickly. A fancy-cut pie of rolled out pie dough was placed on top, and the sides were pinched all round to hold the top and bottom layers together, an art!

75

V.
Again the cookie dough, slightly yeasted, was prepared by the elders who also instructed the younger ladies in the cutting of the cookies and in the shaping of the cookies into flowers, trees, and other shapes. There was creativity and originality in the way the quick fingers shaped almost living things out of the pliant cookie dough. Each admired the other's work.

VI.
After the bread is a golden brown, it is removed with a bread shovel from the oven and placed in traditional baskets. The oven keeper performs this ritual, and the women place the baskets of bread on their heads and carry it to the house. All thirty-six loaves are taken to a room where a lady is down on her hands and knees before a white sheet placed on the floor to receive the loaves for placement on the sheet to cool. Each loaf is handled carefully. Each is positioned in a row of loaves. When the last of the loaves is removed from the oven, it is time to carry out the pies for baking. The pies are placed in the back of the oven with the bread shovel. Cookies are next to the opening, for it takes less time to bake them. The pies and cookies come after the bread is baked because they require less baking time. When the pies and cookies are removed, the pans are placed on the bread boards to be carried to the house. The baking of the bread, pies, and cookies causes those who smell the baking to smile and to be glad. Each has contributed her labor, and each will have her loaf or two of the round, golden loaves, and each will have a pie and some cookies to take home to the family.

MONTANA H. R. WALKING BULL

A Cat and Mouse Story
(Provocation)

The mouse sat still, looking
 at the cat which held the bait.
The cat inched closer, whiskers twitching,
 the bait held tightly in its nervous claws.

The mouse sat still, looking
 at the cat which held the bait.
The cat held the bait close to the mouse's nose,
 dangling it about in the air to tempt him.

The mouse sat still, looking
 at the cat which held the bait.
The cat whispered, Ah, mouse, you are quite a mouse;
 Oh, mouse, I do so like you!

The mouse sat still looking
 at the cat which held the bait.
The cat was now almost upon the mouse whispering,
 Ah, I do so want to know you better.

The mouse's eyes were leveled
 on the cat which held the bait.
The cat's magnetism was working; its whiskers trembling;
 it wouldn't be long now!

The mouse smelled the delicious bait,
 it's nose pressed tight upon it.
The cat's paw was stealthy, quiet, the movement
 to be swift, the mouse already paralyzed.

A cat's spring is quick
A cat killer is quicker
I am the cat killer
I killed the cat that would have eaten
 the mouse that wanted the cheese.

The House of the Seven Frames

We built the first frame on romantic love,
   kisses, closeness and all that.

We built the second frame on silence, wariness,
   suspicion, watchfulness and all that.

We built the third frame on an attempt to see
   just exactly what the other was made of.

We built the fourth frame on weariness, dull
   spirits, and only a glance at each other.

We built the fifth frame on what the hell,
   you go your way and I will go mine.

We built the sixth frame on will he come back,
   and will she have me back if I come home?

We built the seventh frame on something solid,
   a belief in and a love for each other.

MONTANA H. R. WALKING BULL

Going to Market

Do you want to go to market with me, Earl, my brother,
   Do you want to go?
Where is the market, sister, how far away?
It's not far, Earl, my brother, Do you want to go?
Yes, let us go, my sister, but is it very far?
Just about two blocks, my brother, that is all.

Oh, sister, that's a wide street there
   that we have to cross, very wide it is.
It has been such a long time since I have crossed
   a street so very wide.
Cars are going so fast on that wide, wide street.
Oh, sister, please hold my hand.

I will hold your hand, Earl, my brother,
   as we cross the wide, wide street,
   and the cars will not hit you, I will see to that.
Come, take my hand, brother, we will cross together.

Thank you, my sister. I have come from the jungle
   where we fought these many months, and fierce
   it was every day, but not so fierce as this wide,
   wide street and the cars whirling by. Hold my hand.

What Has Happened to Earl's War Medals?

Earl, brother
Earl, singer
Earl, poet
Earl, Marine,

Where are your war medals?

You were sick once in the jungle,
And you sent your white Marine belt home.
We held it in our hands and knew by its length
That you had grown skinny.

You were in the jungle sick and delirious;
You raved in your delirium of thirty fronts
And you wanted someone to look after
Your war medals.
That was when you were sick in the jungle
And someone you didn't know very well
Was looking out for you.

We had a letter about your ravings of thirty fronts
And your concern about your many war medals,
And that was when you sent your white Marine belt home
To let us see how skinny you were.

But all in all, it wasn't noticed so much,
For no one came to you to help you out.
The belt was packed away with the many medals
You had sent home for safekeeping.

Could anyone have helped you then in the jungle?

Now that you are dead,
I can't help wondering where your medals are.
Mama died after she received your dead body from Korea
And placed it alongside our brother Frank at Arlington.
Mama had your portrait done in oils, and it hung in a
Gold frame in the living room. Below it were your medals
in Government issued frames.

But parents die too, Earl, and now I can't help wondering
What has happened to your war medals.

MONTANA H. R. WALKING BULL

You left children too,

Earl, brother
Earl, singer
Earl, poet
Earl, Marine,

And I wonder, what has happened to your children.
They were babies when you were killed in Korea,
And their mother married again and took them away.
They are grown up now somewhere.

You left your medals
And you left your children.
I can't help wondering
What has happened to them.

Willamette Quiet

They come to my house and they say: "It's quiet out here."
The house sits on a hill by a grove of fir trees.
The front faces east to the morning sun.
In the spring the sunrise is a marvel with silhouettes
Of Mt. Hood and Mt. Jefferson dark against blazing reds
Which change to yellow before the sun comes up
From behind the mountain range.

To the north is a twenty-acre farm belonging to a
"Gentleman" farmer who gets chastized regularly by
Old timers because he allows tansy weed to grow and
Permits too much grazing for his animals on too small an acreage.

To the south are a thousand acres owned by a neighbor
Who treats the land with great respect -- every inch of it.
He grows wheat in fenced areas, cuts his oak groves
To thin them out and for firewood against Oregon winters.
He grazes his cattle and sheep in proper enclosures.
He plants new filbert orchards to replace the old.
He sprays from an airplane to kill bugs on cherries,
And he keeps his barns clean. He listens to peacocks
Scream "HALP." He vacations in Arizona at the proper time.

Roadrunners from the college jogging classes practice
Their fancy gaits up and down the road
To improve their posture, their stamina, their bodies.
Girls ride up and down the road exercising their horses and call
    "Hello."

When friends drive out here, they get out of the car,
Look around and say: "It's so quiet out here."

MONTANA H. R. WALKING BULL

Native Son

Towards the soft light of dawn
In the sacred cool of morn,
View the world proudly,
Native son.

With your feet firmly placed
On your Mother, the Earth,
Lift your eyes to your Father,
Native son.

Speak to Wah-kan Tanka
With your head erect,
You are the gift of both,
Native son.

Their child of body and spirit;
They gave you your life,
With pride they acknowledge you,
Native son.

Their union is in you;
The oneness is sacred,
View the world proudly,
Native son.

MONTANA H. R. WALKING BULL

White Buffalo Calf

Young white Buffalo Calf
Frolicking about on the grass,
You are all lovely white, lovely young,
White Buffalo Calf.

You come immediately to my threshold,
Throwing your long body before it,
Holding your graceful head towards the door.
I open the door gingerly, hoping to touch you.

It is then that I notice as I reach out to you
That between your ears is a bow of scarlet
Set against the dazzling white of your head.

Why are you here,
White Buffalo Calf?

MONTANA H. R. WALKING BULL

Grandmother Spider

The picnic's over.
Pieces of food are scattered
about on the ground.

One full sized sandwich
is covered with hundreds
of tiny milling ants.

I pick the sandwich up
to slap at the ants;
they scatter.

I turn the sandwich over
in my hand, and, startled,
throw it down.

A spider under a frothy
feathery web of bread sits
spread out in the center.

Forming a circle around
the spider are small grey ones,
each facing the large spider.

MONTANA H. R. WALKING BULL

The Mission Bell, the Jaguar and the Wrecked Train

Back and forth
the jaguar paces
in the open spaces
around the mission bell
high on the mountain top

In the valley below
I await his quick descent
a zigzagged streak
down the mountain side

And further below
from where I stand
is the wrecked train
the children rode
in the park only yesterday

MONTANA H. R. WALKING BULL

I Touched You and Sparks Flew!

Upon your brow there was a frown;
Beneath your brow an eye crinkled,
   the pupil sliding to one side
   over the arched cheek bone.
You were electric again.
Was there some use then bothering you?

I waited, watched, read the signs,
While you slid to the floor hunting a
   pillow for your head, a prop,
   while you watched teevee, football.
Of course you were electric;
It never failed, your caress.

Time now for me to move in close.
You held the teevee guide in one hand,
   and asked about the time
   and should you get another station.
Your hand, the left one, sought mine.
I touched you and sparks flew!

The Witch

We stood on a steep hill, and down below,
just out of a gulley was a small figure
   weeping loudly.
It cried and cried and cried.
I scrambled down the steep incline
with a thought in my mind
to rescue the weeping child.

I heard someone scream: Don't touch it.
   It's a witch!

By this time, I was on the ground
near the small figure, and I could see
that this was no child.
Its hair was blond, a wig,
worn over an old, old face,
wrinkled and awful.
Its body was small and wiry.
It came towards me, arms outstretched.
Its voice whined and it cried again,
and the eyes glittered and narrowed.

Don't touch it. It's a witch!
The voice cried again in warning.

Now struck with horror, I backed away.
The thing followed me, grinning.
It began to whine again and to cry
very pitifully, but I was wise;
I did not touch it.

MONTANA H. R. WALKING BULL

Propriety
(the big shuck)

Pardon me, but may I take this coke inside?
I'm afraid not, not permitted.
Oh, yes. Well, I'm slowly catching on.
  No eats either, huh?
I'm afraid not, not permitted.
Then I'll move it to where, I wonder?
I'm sorry, no parking room here.
May we use the rest rooms?
I'm afraid not; they are locked.
Oh, yes, I see. How about the drinking fountain?
Yes, if I can find the key. Here.
Please lock it when you are through.
People are so careless.
We have to protect everything;
We have a nice building here
  and want to keep it that way.
I see. Do many people come here?
No, not many, but it's clean.

MONTANA H. R. WALKING BULL

The Mortgage Paid

They were having fun and laughing hard
when suddenly he said,
"I paid your mortgage,
and when I looked into it,
I thought of all those lousy
breakfasts you had prepared
and almost didn't pay it off."

She laughed, teasing,
"Well, I never was much of a cook!"

His mood grew angry.
"I've never eaten such poor food."
He pulled out a knife and glared at her.
"Sometimes I almost want to use this on you.
All that lousy food!"

He held the knife up high ready to strike,
then pulled it back.
"I'm not satisfied with you at all,
but I did pay your mortgage."

MONTANA H. R. WALKING BULL

Stuck With the Color Orange

He was the new University President,
a young one, thirty-six or so.
I entered his office, hesitantly,
when I was struck by the color orange:
a huge orange-colored sofa, bold against
dark walnut paneling and large earthen orange pots,
the color of the desert sunset; brilliant bookends
of orange which sat on the University President's desk.
The windows, clear and bright, showed
a panoramic view of campus and city,
stretching across the long, wide room
of the President's office, six floors up by elevator.
Shelves below the windows were filled with books
to which the President pleasantly referred.
Orange flower pots perched on the top shelf,
bold, bright and defiant! an impressive room,
a room surely designed for austerity,
except that this was a rebellious one.
The color orange spoke out for its occupant:
"Yes, I know, the usual trappings are here,
but behold, there's something else. I am here.
I, a lover of brightness, of life, am here.
Know that brightness shouts above all austerity.
My lot is austerity, for I am the University President,
but I am something else! Hear me!
Let the color orange speak what I cannot."
The new University President, however, apologized.
He apologized for the size of the room;
He apologized for the orange-colored sofa;
He apologized for the orange pots.
"I'm new," he said, "and all this (he waved his hand
and shook his head with a measure of sadness
as he pointed to the colorful objects and
to the largeness of the quarters designed to
to house the University President), all this," he
continued, "was the arrangement made by my predecessor."

MONTANA H. R. WALKING BULL

Death Trap

I saw you build my death trap.
Yes, I stood and watched you
so carefully construct the part
right in front of my door
that would collapse
as I crossed the threshold.

You made it round and brown and firm,
though it sank slightly in the middle.
It looked porous and crepy and thin.
You were a craftsman, so carefully
did you build it, seam upon seam,
a tidy job, with all edges sealed and trim.
Yes, I witnessed the building
of my own death trap.
And you were merry as you whistled and
tucked in the corners.
It must be a good one to fool me!

But I was the watcher, and I was calm
as I saw you there on your knees before it,
measuring and fixing, and patting it down,
So you couldn't know, could you,
that as you stood back to appraise
your job well done, that
it was your death trap too?

MONTANA H. R. WALKING BULL

Out of a Portland Hilton Hotel Window

The Congress Hotel and River Room,
Hertz Rent-a-Car and seven layers
  of parking space.
Pacific Power and I. Magnin & Co.,
The American flag dead center on top
  of the building
Rising high on its pole and blowing
  in the Oregon wet breeze.

Trailways with thru bus signs,
A swimming pool set in a cement patio floor,
A fir tree rising two floors
  straight up from the cement.

The U. S. National Bank, Metropolitan Branch,
A pine potted in a cement bowl,
Metal chairs turned upside down
  beside the deserted pool
  where raindrops scar the water.

A bus stops to load its passengers,
  and cars, all colors, all makes,
  move slowly only one way.

The American flag,
The State of Oregon flag,
The H. Hilton flag,
  billow in the Oregon wind.

Plants edge the outdoor patio
  against iron railings.
Three hundred windows across the street
On the bold facade of the Pacific Power building
  show people moving about
  among machines, clocks,
  and fluorescent lights.

The city and the Portland Hilton Hotel.

Hope

In a square built house
Old, old, old,
Lives Hope.

In a shapeless dress
With a toothless smile
And stringy hair
Is Hope.

In an ill kept lawn
By a garden small
Near a Jersey cow
Stands Hope.

Happy, hearty Hope.

MONTANA H. R. WALKING BULL

In Early Morning

Lacy, white and shimmering,
The threads are spun
Between the green painted
Wrought-iron railings.

Intricately designed, they follow
The rails in repetition across the bridge.

They shine and glimmer in the dew against
The eastern sun as they wait for prey.

Lurking unnoticed, but aware and still,
Is the lone and patient spider
Ready to take that which sustains.

Oh, lovely webs,
Oh, darksome spider,
Alas, the unwary catch,
Its struggle useless.

So brave the flight that dooms.

MONTANA H. R. WALKING BULL

The Sickness

Ego mania
  gobbles,
  devours,
  turns forever
  inward.

Its concentration
  is self.
It wants sacrifices
  to itself.
It wants continued
  support.
It cannot stand
  alone without
  its food--
  others--
  which it eats,
  greedily.

Those who withstand
  its appetite,
  it hates.
It demands that
  everyone
  focus upon
  itself.

It talks about itself.
It finds what it says
  important,
  fascinating,
  alive,
  brilliant.

It makes of itself
  an oracle,
  a sage,
  a prophet
  a seer.

MONTANA H. R. WALKING BULL

It prattles,
  uselessly,
  creating a
  vast boredom
  in others.

It scintillates
  as it caresses
  itself
  and croons
  to itself
  and exalts
  itself.

What manner
  of doctor
  can cure
  a sickness
  that demands
  of others
  the living
  sacrifice?

Sacrifice to
  what?
  A vacuum?
  A non being?
  A living farce?

MONTANA H. R. WALKING BULL

The Loner

It stands alone, small and black
Between two white fence posts.
It faces the wind and the rain
Standing still, its head up.
It knows its domain, three acres.
It knows its refuge, the fir grove.
It flies like the crow, its neighbor,
When it hears the bark of a dog.
It hatches its eggs and sits on them
In the barn, year in and year out,
But nothing comes of it,
For there's no rooster.
It has high hopes, this
Stalwart black bantam hen, and
It has survived the dog and the fox
For six long years.

MONTANA H. R. WALKING BULL

From the Wilderness

From the wilderness the voice crying,
"What shall we do about our future?"
The answer ready, toneless and final,
"We'll live it, I guess."
Too often the subject broached,
The puzzle unsolved and ignored,
A life lived on the narrow edge of nowhere;
A path, barren and sombre.
Dead leaves blow about them,
Chilled winds press close upon them
While the struggle for understanding
Is forever closed by the clamp
Of the hollow, ready answer,
"We'll live it, I guess,"
And dry eyes stare at the ceiling.

99

MONTANA H. R. WALKING BULL

Youth

My radiant company
Is not among the aging.
I run with lightning speed
On a moonlit night.
I have an unbearable ache for a lover
And the solace of my dreams.
My hours are idled away.
Oh, the world is a glory;
It cannot last long;
It will last forever in a song.

There is no age for youth but youth,
All else is a blur in time.
Winter is spring; there is no fall,
And the mirror proves it all.

I am the strong!
Sorrow only is long.

MONTANA H. R. WALKING BULL

The Pity of It All

It was just impossible.
Oh, me;
Oh, Bud.
Poor little Bud.
Sweet, innocent, little Bud,
So trusting, so believing,
What I did to him!
Why didn't I stop
While there was time?

And his mother, his sweet mother,
Going more than half way.
What I did to her!
Oh, why didn't I stop?

And these children,
These poor little children
Being taken in on things.
And doing the very thing
I knew was wrong
And not stopping
And going on.

You know what I did,
Don't you know what I mean?
Oh, oh--
After pulling him down
And these children
And knowing when
I should have stopped,
And with these babies
And all my family,
Oh, oh--

MONTANA H. R. WALKING BULL

A Nice Looking Boy

Bert was in the bathroom again. He had been there for thirty minutes, and Katherine knew he would be there for thirty minutes more if past experience counted for anything. What a price to pay for appearance, she thought. No doubt he would be combing his sleek, black hair over and over until it gleamed. How carefully he must work to press the one large wave in place above his high forehead.

Katherine's process of thought came to an abrupt close when Bert suddenly threw open the bathroom door. Without a glance at the girl at the table, he walked past her into her bedroom. She was bent over drawings of moths and butterflies, carefully inspecting the fine lines and tracings.

She felt his presence near her before he spoke. His dark, handsome face, she knew, was cold and impassive above her. She saw with her head bent low over the table, out of the corner of one eye, his immaculately shined shoes and the cuffs of trousers newly creased. She smelled the cleanness of his body.

"I want your face powder," he said with cold, precise enunciation. "Where it it?"

To emphasize her contempt for him and his vain interest in himself, she continued to write the caption under a picture, trying hard to keep her hand from shaking.

"I haven't any powder. I'm out," she said.

"That's a lie! You got a new box yesterday. I saw it," he said. She saw then his tightly clenched fists and white knuckles.

"The new box is lost," she said. "I can't find it anywhere." She didn't look at him when she told him. The caterpillar on the page above her caption loomed larger and she saw details on the drawing she hadn't noticed before as she stared at it fixedly.

Katherine knew if she looked at Bert he could read the lie on her face. He would be able to review her action of hiding the face powder. He would hit her. She kept her eyes averted, and he went back into her bedroom. She heard him throwing things around. To escape witnessing the destruction of her possessions and to maintain control, she left as quietly as she could and went outside. She hid behind the woodpile in the strawberry patch. As she squatted down and picked some of the red, juicy berries she watched the house for some sign of Bert. She wondered why this brother of hers always bathed himself in perfumed water and why he used her bath powder afterwards during his sixty minutes of "fixing" himself before he went out. She suspected him of using her face powder too, and that's why she hid it from him -- to find out for sure.

MONTANA H. R. WALKING BULL

When it was safe for Katherine to go back into the house, she left her place of refuge. She had seen Bert leave dressed in the new suit their father could not afford to buy. She had questioned the source of his funds until she found the study desk with the roll top gone. Bert took it to the second-hand man and sold it for fifteen dollars. She saw her mother cry over the new rug Bert took from the floor and sold the week her father was out of town. It was the first rug her mother had bought since Ron was a baby, but Bert looked nice in the suit. He was a nice looking boy. Everyone who saw him in it said so. Her mother said nothing to Bert. Katherine could picture quite another scene when her father returned home. The day Bert sold the rug, her mother stood at the window and looked out towards the mountains and cried.

At the far end of the stack of wood Katherine saw Bert drive away in the shiny car which he wouldn't let anyone else in the family touch. Her father was away from home so much he hardly knew what went on. He couldn't know that Bert drove the car all the time. Even in the cold of the Oregon winter when Katherine and her younger brother, Ron, walked a mile and a half to high school through tunnels of deep snow piled up on either side of the sidewalk, Bert, in their father's car, was on his way to attend his college classes on the hill. Bert always followed close behind the snow plows so his way would be clear. Sometimes he stopped near where Katherine and Ron walked and beckoned them to the car. After they climbed laboriously up over the snowbank to the road where Bert parked, he pressed on the starter and drove away leaving them stranded. He rolled his window down quickly, stuck his head out, laughing and yelling about how funny they looked standing there after missing their ride. Katherine and Ron stood looking after their elder brother, their hair turning frosty white under their caps as they stood silently in the cold. They tried to push their hair back under their woolen caps. They looked at each other, vaguely waiting, disbelief mingled with wonder, but they didn't talk about it.

While Katherine watched with amazement and a fine contempt at the way Bert operated, she knew in her heart that this kind of chicanery which he employed so naturally and artfully would fit him admirably for the world in which he was sure to make a mark.

Katherine hated Bert's insides while she did without so he could have the things he wanted and demanded. She grew used to his passing her on the street in her shabbiness when he failed to recognize her as his sister.

At last she pulled herself up from the ground and decided to face the damage in her room.

Every drawer had its contents emptied on the floor. She could picture every deliberate movement he must have made. Blouses, brassieres, panties, letters, pictures, bobby pins, handkerchiefs, little keepsakes, all were dumped together in an indescribable mess on the floor. Sheets were in shreds on the bed. She found the bedspread wadded up and stuck behind the dresser. Torn curtains billowing and blowing out into the room were half off the bent rods. With a clean sweep he had knocked her poor array of cosmetics off the dresser and onto the floor. One precious bottle of toilet water was gone. Clothes ripped from hangers in the closet had footmarks where he had stomped them in his wrath.

She might have wept, but recurrent scenes with Bert had made her impervious to tears. The only way to save pride was to seek revenge. He must be punished for his crime.

Bert's room was locked. She jimmied it open. Everything in his sanctuary was in perfect order and clean the way he liked to have it. No one trespassed in his room. Katherine tried to open the dresser drawers, but they were secure. The desk was locked. She got a screw driver from the back porch and pried the top of the desk open, leaving ugly broken places at the sides where she gouged at the wood.

"There are probably pictures of his girl friends in here," she said. "He goes out almost every evening."

Not a single picture. She took plenty of time to examine every crook and cranny of the desk. No letters, only a small address book neatly wrapped in tissue paper. She had expected something more exciting than the little book with all the trouble she went to. Two bottles of ink were more than half full. She opened the tiny book and saturated it page by page with red and green ink. The last name blotted out was Stan.

While Kaherine worked, she began to get whiffs of her mother's cooking from the other end of the house. She left Bert's room and walked down the long hall and out into the cooking part of the large old-fashioned house. Her mother stood at the stove stirring meat and vegetables in a large kettle. Some people called what her mother made hash, but the special way Katherine's mother made it with lots of potatoes, huge hunks of beef, strong-flavored with whole onions, big slices of carrots, cuts of green peppers and hot red peppers if she could buy them, cabbage and peas, they called it vegetable soup. It was Katherine's favorite food and she knew she wouldn't get any for supper.

"Mother," she said, "Bert and I had some trouble today while you were out. I think I'd better spend the night with Inez. You don't need to tell Bert where I've gone. He'll be angry with me."

"I won't tell him," her mother said. She sighed a great, deep sigh, and the look of sorrow and sadness came into her dark eyes. "You go ahead, Katherine. It's about all you can do if you've had trouble again."

Her mother stirred the vegetables and placed the lid on top.

"I don't know why you children can't get along," she said. "It might be different if your father were here."

"It's the way Bert acts and the way he treats me," Katherine said.

"Bert isn't like you and Ronnie. He's different." Her mother looked out the kitchen window. She held the long-handled spoon in her hand and had that far-away look she always got when she talked about her nice looking boy.

Picture of a Family

"Why don't you go over to see Mrs. Bishop while you are home?" Canna's mother said. She held a pair of shrubbery clippers in her hand. An old pair of faded jeans hung on her full hips, the side zipper not quite meeting the band over the bulge of her waist. The pants were so disreputable that Canna was ashamed for her.

"You wear those ragged pants all the time," the girl said. "They look awful."

Canna had mowed the lawn on the side of the late Victorian brick house which was her parents' home. She was busy with the front, pushing the heavy motorless mower towards the tight wire fence when her mother called from the porch which led half way around the house.

Canna stopped, leaned on the handle and puffed, her breath coming in short gasps. A hot blister had formed on her heel underneath the canvas shoes. A corn on the little toe of the left foot underneath a medicated plaster burned with pain.

Her mother's reply was curt. "What I wear is all right. I don't care anything about it. Nobody sees me. I don't care how I look."

Canna walked over to the step and sat down where she faced the highway. Cars went by lickity-split to Wallowa Lake. The people inside the cars looked fierce and determined as though they meant to escape what they had left behind them at all costs. It was a nice summer day.

"You always suggest that I should go over and see the Bishops when I'm here," Canna complained.

"I told Mrs. Bishop you would see her. Her husband is sick again. I said you would go by to see him," her mother said.

Canna threw her cotton gloves to the ground. "Why did you tell her that? It's plain what's on your mind-- what's under that crafty, but lovable face of yours. You never give up, do you? Let me tell you. You can't stand to see that I'm single and that I'm a little old to still be without a husband. You would like to see me make a match with Gordon and be the proud possessor of the Bishop farms. Isn't that really it?"

Her mother laughed while she leaned against the white round post which led up towards the intricate woodcut floral pattern that lifted and dipped around the porch.

"Mebbe so. Still, why do you have to be so cutting and so bitter too. Life needn't ever become that serious. You're too young for it. Isn't the shade of those big old trees nice? They give us shade all around the porch."

MONTANA H. R. WALKING BULL

"It's just that I don't like being reminded of Gordon every time I come home, and I don't like having to go there either." Canna pushed the soft earth with the heel of her rubber sole.

"You make me tired. What's the matter with you, anyway?" her mother said. She leaned back, grasping the edge of the porch to keep herself steady.

"I don't know why you can't see -- or maybe you do. It's always the same there. They never change. They haven't changed since I first knew them."

"That's a stupid way to look at it," her mother said. "They're just like the rest of us. Well, you don't **have** to go." She picked up the clippers and went into the house.

With extreme reluctance Canna walked down the short path to the gate. She opened the catch and followed the narrow worn path for two blocks until she came to the corner where a large white frame house stood back from the road. She noticed they weren't keeping the weeds down.

Phyllis sat in her regular place on the screened in front porch. She called a hello from her wheelchair and pulled off the scarf from her head to wave a welcome. She wheeled over to open the door for Canna. Mr. Bishop lay just inside the open door which led to the living room. His hand and arm were hidden beneath a large heating pad. With his free hand he waved feebly to Canna.

She walked over to him. "How are you, Mr. Bishop? How are you feeling?"

He smiled, a labored crooked smile, and said, "Oh, well, I guess. How are you?"

"Oh, fine," she laughed.

Mrs. Bishop came into the parlor from the kitchen. Her hair was in disarray, her arthritic, gnarled fingers smoothed down the apron over her protruding stomach. Then she took Canna's hand and pressed it warmly. Canna felt the hard, calloused mounds and the enlarged bones.

"Sit down, won't you? We are so glad to see you. How is everything in Salem. Your mother says you are still working at the capitol building."

"Yes, still plugging away. How are things with you?"

Mrs. Bishop laughed. "As long as the doctor keeps me doped up, I can keep going. Gordon's not been so good though. Been sick with the flu. Phyllis' eyes are in bad shape. We've been doctoring right along." She spoke with a nervous, spasmodic laugh which interspersed her words. With the laughter was the accompanying twitch of her body.

Canna followed the crippled girl's eyes as they kept shifting over to where her father's long lean body stretched out on the couch. The look was anxious with a kind of timeless expression of love and sympathy in it.

107

Canna thought of the lifetime of despair in the large, gray eyes which sought those of the disabled father. Phyllis had been forty years in a wheelchair with legs never developed enough to carry the weight of her body. Canna saw knowledge in eyes fading with age and long loneliness -- knowledge of what the wheelchair had meant to the gray-haired arthritic mother who sat in the same chair vicariously for forty years -- knowledge of what it meant to her to have the kind, good father who now and always bore his suffering with the sweet smile. The next stroke would surely take the feeble life away, the life of a father in despair because his only daughter would never walk in her lifetime.

The knowledge which was manifested in the eyes of Phyllis overwhelmed Canna and made her feel weak and insufficient. It was the sorrow she saw in them that such things are or can be. She sensed in their all-knowing look the effect of her confinement on the sacrificial family. Whose doing was all this, Canna wondered. The question showed too in those large gray eyes in the large head showing the ravages of age, the head attached to a worthless body by a scrawny, wrinkled neck. Some power to which they all must bend was present here, and it had imprisoned Phyllis, Gordon and the father and mother.

Canna's mind turned to Gordon, the man who might have been her husband, but who could never be because he was bound to the family. She thought of the toll of the years, remembering him as he had looked when she first met him many years ago. He had said to her then that he must work hard because of the family. The pattern had been set.

She remembered Mrs. Bishop's saying to her mother, "Sometimes we get so blue, but we have to be cheerful to keep Phyllis' spirits up." And there was Mr. Bishop saying at the postoffice every morning as he waited for his mail, "Yes, we are all getting along fine." And there was Gordon's slience that ran on through the years. He tilled the vast Bishop fields, gathered the harvest, bred his fine stock and put away money for the family's security. He now worked alone since his father's stroke.

Canna looked towards the dining room. "What pretty dishes," she said, looking at the china on display in the china closet.

"Want to see them?" Mrs. Bishop asked. Canna followed her through the wide, high doorway into the room filled with heavy oak furniture.

"You haven't seen my dishes, have you?" she asked.

"No. Mother thinks they are lovely. She's always talking about your nice things. I would love to see them," Canna said.

"They aren't much, I'm sure," Mrs. Bishop said as she let the younger woman examine the china lined up in full view on shelves protected behind glass. The dishes were dusty. She apologized while she explained to Canna where each dish originated.

Phyllis wheeled herself in through the doorway and waited. Canna held a hand-painted plate up to the light and commented on the artistry, directing her remarks to the girl in the chair as well. Canna thought of Phyllis as a girl, though she was middle-aged, but what had she known beyond girlhood? Phyllis still held the silk scarf in her hands moving it back and forth between her fingers feeling its softness, listening attentively to Canna's superficial remarks.

"If you really like old things, let me show you this beautiful mahogany dresser which came from our old home in Philadelphia," Mrs. Bishop said as she led Canna to the bedroom.

In the corner stood a massive dresser with wide flawless mirror.

"It's cedar lined," Mrs. Bishop said, as she opened the drawers. She began to display the embroidered linens in the first long drawer. When she had finished with them, she opened the bottom drawer and there were the family pictures. Mrs. Bishop and her husband at the turn of the century, she with a large hat and plumes beneath which was an austere face, a high collar and a big bosom.

"I was a secretary when I met Mr. Bishop," she explained.

Mr. Bishop as a high school graduate stood on the back row with his class, the men in white stiff collars, their hair parted in the middle and slicked down; the girls in white tight shirtwaists, long full skirts, leaning languidly against one another in a soft, graceful, carefully-studied informal pose.

There was a picture of Phyllis and Gordon. The little girl's dress was lavishly embroidered. She wore a big, wide bow of ribbon on top of her head. Her chubby body sat on a small table. Her short, undeveloped stems, on which she could never stand, hung uselessly down. Gordon stood, a younger, brave soldier-like figure, stalwart and protecting, by his sister's side.

"You were a sweet, little thing," Canna said to Phyllis.

"Oh, yes," she said. "I was fat too. And look at how fat Gordon is. He was a fat little thing, too."

The grandmother's quilt lay at the foot of the bed. Mrs. Bishop sat on it and talked. Her mattress was so high on the bed that her feet couldn't reach the floor. Canna sat in a straightbacked chair and heard about their winter's illnesses.

Mrs. Bishop's laugh was noisy and shrill. "Oh, I don't know what will ever become of us," she said. We had Dad in the hospital two days and they said he was in good shape, but I don't know. Gordon took us in to get him last night after the field work was done. And almost as soon as we got up this morning Dad began to complain that his hand was going dead on him. He couldn't move his fingers. Right away I called one of the neighbors to try to locate Gordon who had been gone since daylight. He came in from the field and we drove back to town, but the doctor couldn't figure it out. He sent us back home and told me to keep Dad's hand warm. We've had the hot pad on it all morning. I just don't know what to think anymore. These hospitals cost so much money. Dad said they didn't feed him much either. He told me exactly what was on his tray, and it wasn't much. Still, they certainly charge you enough, goodness knows. Sickness sure costs. It wouldn't be so bad if they'd just tell you what's wrong, but they don't say a thing to give you any satisfaction. We had Phyllis to Pendleton for an eye test. She can't see very well out of one eye, she says."

"It's my left eye," Phyllis said as she rubbed it.

"The doctor didn't tell me a thing. I got the prescription filled, but I don't know whether it helped her or not. Still, he charged plenty."

"Then," Mrs. Bishop went on, "Gordon's been ailing with flu off and on all winter. When he don't have that, it's his hay fever, but he's like me -- got to keep going. The reason I stay up is that I've got dope for my arthritis. As long as I get a couple of shots a day I can stay up and about."

As Canna listened to the monologue, she wondered if Phyllis was aware of the stringy, thin gray hair, the deeply-wrinkled face, the body misshapen with work, the fingers gnarled and swollen. Yet from the mother's eyes came the unexpected twinkle, the hearty laugh, while she related their daily tragedies.

Mrs. Bishop slid off the bed when she heard a knock at the back door, and Canna took the opportunity to say she must leave.

"I think I will slip out the front door. I hope my visit hasn't disturbed your father too much," she said to Phyllis.

"Of course not," Phyllis said. "Don't hurry off."

Mr. Bishop lay quietly on the couch as Canna started to pass by. She thought he was asleep. He raised himself, his face alight with hope and faith that he would be better soon.

"Look," he said. He held his troubled hand up. "I can wiggle my fingers."

"I am so glad," Canna said. "It's not much fun to be sick, is it?"

"No, is isn't much fun," he said sadly, looking out the window at weeds grown up around the house. "I can't get anything done this way."

Canna walked down the steps of the Bishop home and thought about the shadowy figure of Gordon who at this moment was at work in the field. A man of the soil. Gordon with his miserable hay fever. She thought of the lively young man she had known when he exhibited his stock at the state fair the year he won all the prizes and the difference a few years had made.

Gordon had become the shadow of a human being, his being slowly ebbing away, his hair thin and turning grey, his only friend and companion a dog. What things he must say to the dog which no human ear could attend. Not even the woman he loved, but would not take, knew what dreams he might have dreamed before he realized the shackles he wore.

His dreams had died a long time ago, the only remembrance of dreams of love would be stolen stealthily in fear of family betrayal. It would be only those moments while he sat in the farm truck before an evening meal presided over by a worrying, sick mother, or in the faintness of an early dawn when he awoke for another day's toil in his fields, or the lift of his gaze to the lofty Mt. Emily, covered with dense forests below the blue of the Eastern Oregon sky and the fleecy white clouds which hover over the colored landscape -- only the moments when the call of the bird, or the memory of a girl's sweet song could stir his soul, only these moments could perhaps sustain him in his peril.

How is Clara?

Outside the house were two small boys, playing and romping with their dog in the dirty yard piled with junk and old empty beer bottles and cans. Their mother's shadowy face watched from the window. Her figure showed she was burdened with the child she soon would bear, and her features were marked with despondency.

The woman was small, undernourished and colorless. Neglected hair in dry strings fell about her pointed pinched face. An unironed blouse hung half out of her skirt which was pulled up to one side and hitched together with a safety pin.

Shoulders were hunched with a perpetual droop and her legs protruded awkwardly from the dirty skirt she wore. Swollen feet slopped about in faded sneakers when she walked. A cigarette dangled from her lips.

Blatant music shot out of a cheap record player with "Detour, There's a Muddy Road Ahead." Clara stopped the needle at the finish. Her cigarette burned into the table where it lay forgotten.

Bill, her husband, was in the kitchen opening another can of beer. He brought in two glasses and handed her one filled with the beer. He sat down and grunted.

"What you plan to do with them kids' presents?"

"I haven't thought about it yet," Clara said.

"Could burn 'em," the man said sipping his beer and looking at his wife over the top of his glass.

"No," she turned away. "I don't want to burn them."

"I don't get it," the man said. He propped his feet on a small wooden stool and leaned back to enjoy the beer.

Clara's feet ached. She put the glass of beer on the table and sat down heavily in a chair, involuntarily placing both hands below the large bulge to support herself. She sighed. "Doug's parents have always liked the kids," she said.

"I wouldn't brag about it," he snapped. "Now go ahead and drink that beer. It's no good if it sets awhile!"

"That's what you always say. I'm not bragging. You brought the subject up."

"Send them back to the old fogies. That's what I say. Send 'em back and show them how we feel about their charity!" Bill got up, scratched the middle of his back and walked back into the kitchen.

Clara sat while she tried to sip the beer, but it didn't taste good. She put the glass down and thought about the father of the two boys out playing in the yard. Doug was dead. She thought she couldn't go on after he was killed in Korea. She remembered how she cried for days and days and how everything during that time lost its meaning for her including the two little boys. In desperation she took the boys, who were only babies then, back to Doug's folks. She thought about Doug's mother and remembered how she had cried too when there was any mention about Doug. His mother would look at the children and cry some more. Clara couldn't stand it.

Doug's pictures were on the mantle above the fireplace in his mother's house. A large oil painting of Doug in Marine uniform hung on the wall of the living room. While she lived in his mother's house, his eyes were always on her, watching. In his Marine dress uniform he watched and waited to see what she would do now that he was dead. She got to where she couldn't stand living there. She left and bought a little place to be by herself.

It was lonely.

Now, after a year of marriage with Bill, she was still lonely. She couldn't forget Doug. She remembered his moods, his quiet ways, his silly attempts to write poetry for the Leatherneck Magazine, and how happy he was when they were published. She remembered the seriousness with which he took out as much insurance as he was allowed so that she and the boys might not suffer, just in case . . .

Now she was cut off from Doug's people. It was still hard to believe that all the insurance money was gone. Bill had quickly spent all the money, and they were in debt.

Clara went to the window again. Her boys. Would Doug recognize them with their hair uncut, their clothes ragged and dirty? Although Doug was a Protestant, he hadn't objected when the priest baptised the children. She walked over to the table where the packages lay. Two little corduroy shirts from Doug's parents. She carefully folded the shirts and placed them back in their wrappings.

Questions flooded her mind leaving her dizzy. Why did Doug have to be killed? Why had she married Bill? What was ahead? She remembered a chance remark which had been attributed to Bill. "Somebody's going to marry the widow and use up all that money, and it might as well be me!"

She looked down at her big shoes and her swollen feet. "Everyone in town looks down on me. They look away when I pass them on the street. I could stand almost anything if they just would stop calling me up and playing the Marine Hymn on the phone. They play that and hang up. I wonder who is doing that to me."

That night Clara lay awake in bed thinking again. "I wish I didn't think at all. My head aches when I worry, and it gets worse if I keep fretting."

It had got to be a habit. She would wake up at all times of the night to wonder about her life. She would get tired of not being able to sleep and would throw her pillow on the floor, lie quietly for a little while and try again to go to sleep, but the movements of the baby disturbed her. She would turn from side to side to find a comfortable position, but there was none. This time she got up to go to the bathroom, her water broke, and it scared her. It was like a bucket turned over. She went back to the bed where Bill lay snoring loudly.

She shook him, "Bill, get up. Get up, Bill!" She shook him again, and he grunted, half awake. He sat up finally and ran his hands through his hair.

"Damndest time to wake a man up," he said, "What's the matter with you?"

"My water's broke."

Clara lay back down on the bed and gazed straight up at the ceiling, for the slight cramps had begun.

Bill eased out from under the cover and pulled on his pants. He got his coat on and turned to his wife.

"I'll get the doctor," he said, and he left.

Near the bed on a chipped and dusty table lay a magazine. Clara took it in her hands and tried to read. The pains came at quicker intervals, but she could read a little between the pains. As they got harder, she scrunched her body up and groaned. When they got very hard, she pushed her perspiring head against the pillow and screamed.

The children heard her. They came into the room, stood by her bed and began to cry. "What's the matter, mommy?" She took no notice of them.

Bill came back and tried to shove the boys out of the room when he saw her writhing on the bed. The boys wouldn't leave. They stood at the door rubbing their backsides against the frame and cried softly.

"Is the doctor here?" Clara asked hoarsely.

"He's here," said Bill. "Christ, does it hurt that much?"

"Get the kids out," she cried with the heavy push of the pain.

The doctor came in with the nurse, and Bill took the children out of the room.

Clara knew there is nothing in life or death to compare with this. In the haze of the pain she saw the nurse as she bent over her to press something into her mouth. There was a glass of water which she drank.

She was conscious of the clean sheets which were swathed about her; she felt her limbs being lifted and her arms strapped to her sides. She felt the swabbing of merthiolate.

"Bear hard with the pain, little mother," the nurse urged softly as she placed a rubber cup close to Clara's nose. "Bear down hard on the pain and breathe deeply, little mother," the nurse spoke again.

Clara tried to work with the pain. As she pushed with it her eyes fell upon the dusty crucifix on the wall near the bed. It was one which her mother had given her years ago. Now as she looked at it, she saw as though for the first time its clear beauty. It was the figure of the Lord Jesus Christ, Son of the Blessed Virgin. She saw the detail of

Christ's suffering and his agony on the cross, the nails through His hands and feet, the bleeding wounds, the hanging head with the heavy wreath of thorns. If He could bear such suffering, she could bear hers. Clara bore with the pain, for the Blessed Son had given her peace. As it flowed gently into her being there was the strength to bear her own agony. She breathed into the mask placed on her face and felt herself sucked into a colored spiral that sang as she descended.

"How is Clara?"

"She died early this morning after giving birth to a fine baby girl."

And someplace, a distance away, someone was dialing a number to play the Marine Hymn.

Survival

Lewis Mumford said something in his book, **Values for Survival**, to indicate that as long as we allow our emotions to dictate what we are to do, or if we let subjectivity take priority over objectivity, as we seem to have done up to now, then we can never have any particular kind of a real progress as human beings because things of a subjective nature are stumbling blocks to progress and serve only as hindrances.

This point of view interested me, especially at this time, because it has seemed to me that when I have experienced hurt that is of an emotional nature, it is a kind of death agony--a kind of prolonged dying which finally is over and when it is gone, it leaves me cut out and hollow inside. I have often thought how much better off I would be if it were possible for me to so regulate my own mind, get it into some kind of channel where it would be impervious to pain. But I have not arrived at that point yet. I think that I will not let anything or anyone affect me, yet I do, and when I go down into the darkness of despair, there surely is no one who can sink lower. Death surely isn't any worse.

There is a deadening quality about such despair. It is as though I am drowning and can't get up for air. The amazing thing about this is that (if there isn't the attempt to take life or to do something equally drastic during the suffering period) one does survive. I rise up again in all my splendor and life is good again. The sun shines, and I am alive once more, able to see, to laugh, to hope, and eventually, I tell myself the emotion of love will come again. Sometime again I will know the glory, the pain and agony of love even though I have turned my back on the thought during the pain and even after the pain.

But to get back to objectivity. That, it seems to me, is the answer. If I don't feel, I won't be hurt. If I don't love, I won't be hurt. If I don't care for anyone, I won't be hurt.

For it seems to me that the minute a person cares, he is sunk! If he doesn't care, nothing another person says or does will make any difference. Then we rule out love. If we rule out love, what is there between a man and a woman? Physical satisfaction or needs met, as one eats when one is hungry and rests when one is tired. Key words are routine and necessity, but these are not to affect us emotionally.

Marriage is essential, if for no other reason than that it serves as good therapy -- and everyone to be sound needs this kind of therapy. Not all ills are alleviated, though some are. There's someone to listen when one talks. There's someone to look to the other's needs. There's someone to lean on, someone to talk to, someone to be with physically. There's also the aura of nice respectability about marriage which not many want to challenge. Without these needs met, there is a sense of loss. The fact is, man needs woman, and the two make a whole. Even the poorest marriage, I believe, is better than no marriage at all. In marriage too, in order to eliminate pain, leave emotion out of it. Just let it be a cut and dried proposition (it eventually comes to that anyway), and anything one does or says will be all right. The other person or partner will not be affected. But if a person cares a little, if he or she is weak, subjective, emotional, and if either cares a little about the other person, see the difference it makes!

There seems to be a sadistic streak in us which causes us to attack those who show any sign of weakness. We like to crush the life out of the weak and throw the remains on the rubbish heap. But if one doesn't care, if no one cares, there's no pain, and life can be lovely. (Sorry, can't use the word lovely; it's emotional). Without emotion there can be no suffering. Let us rid ourselves of this stumbling block to human interaction and look to real progress as human beings. If Mumford's idea of eliminating subjectivity (which also gets rid of God, any values connected with religion, anything connected with the spirit or soul of man), then we can indeed begin to live in a brave new world.

Notes on Cherokees and Sioux

Glossary of Sioux Words and Phrases Used in the Text With English Meanings

THE CHEROKEES

It is said that "The Cherokee story is proof that humanity will not only endure but triumph."

Cherokees settled in North and South Carolina, Tennessee and northern Georgia, though their beginnings are not known. They were the largest group of Indians in the southeast when the white man encountered them. By 1820, their eastern holdings were considerably reduced by white intrusion and those who had not yet been moved west were moved in 1838 and joined the Cherokees already settled in Indian Territory (Arkansas and Oklahoma). Eventually most of the Arkansas Cherokees were moved to what is now Oklahoma. The Cherokees in northern Georgia and Tennessee were moved by the U. S. Military on orders of Andrew Jackson. This move is called the "Trail of Tears," for of the last 16,000 moved, 4,000 perished on the way. Frontier contact dated from 1540 to 1785; white ascendancy, from 1768 to 1828; tribal dislocation from 1829 to 1846; the struggle for self-government, from 1847 to 1860; American Civil War and Reconstruction, from 1861 to 1867; establishment of the Cherokee Nation, from 1867 to 1892, and termination and statehood, 1893 to 1907.

Cherokees, at the insistence of both Washington and Jefferson, forged themselves into a political state. This was for the purpose of survival. They adopted a written constitution, had their own alphabet, their own printing presses and papers in their own language after Sequoyah invented the Cherokee alphabet, and as a nation in Oklahoma established their own educational institutions to educate their men and women equally. Before the move to the west, they fought to maintain their eastern homes through the courts of law, but Andrew Jackson forced the move west even over the objection of John Marshall who had affirmed the legal position of the Cherokees in the east.

Reference: Rennard Strickland. **Fire and the Spirits** -- Cherokee Law from Clan to Court. University of Oklahoma Press, Norman, Oklahoma, 1975.

THE TETON SIOUX

The Teton Sioux call themselves **Lakota,** meaning "allies." There were seven main divisions called the Seven Council Fires. Several of these were further divided into bands. For example, the Teton Sioux (Lakota) were divided into Brules (both upper and lower), the Hunkpapa, the Minicoujou, the Oglala, the Oahenonpa or Two Kettle, the Sans Arcs, and the Sihasapa or Blackfoot.

The Sioux nation was the largest of the Plains Indian groups, and they once lived (it is believed) on the Atlantic Coast. They went west and lived in southern Minnesota, in Iowa and in Wisconsin (before these territories were states), and they finally settled on the great Plains where they dominated over a territory from Canada to the Platte River, from Minnesota to the Yellowstone River including the Black Hills and the Powder River country.

The Sioux are known for their courage, their high intelligence, their beauty of form, their resourcefulness and their accomplishments. Their fashions and regalia are unequalled, and they excel in decoration, in quill and bead work. Their colorful geometric designs have religious significance. They were well known for their society, its organization, and their religious rites. They are visionaries. In war they were much feared, and when they faced the U.S. Military, they fought bravely and brilliantly to protect their land and their people against the enemy.

Today Sioux leaders are found everywhere in American life. They are excellent writers (Vine Deloria, Jr.), speakers (Bea Medicine), thinkers (Lame Deer), and are perhaps best known for their music, their singers and drummers, such as Oglala singers: William Horncloud, Ben Sitting Up, and Frank Afraid of Horses, as well as Matthew Two Bulls and singers called "The Sons of the Oglalas."

Sioux fashions (regalia) always have been an inspiration to Indians everywhere.

Glossary of Sioux Words and Phrases
Used in the Text

Ca-oo (He's coming)

Chan-te T-in-za (Brave Heart Man)

Hau, or Ha-oo (Hello, or So it shall be--according to its use in the sentence)

Hau kola, or Hou-kola (Hello, friend)

Heh wah-shi ah man-u (One who steals tallow from that old woman)

Ho, a-sni-kiya yo (Rest your strength)

Ho he che-tu we-lo (So it is indeed, or So it has been said, or So it has been told)

Ho i-ya yo, or Ho-ee ya yo (Well, let us go)

ho-pi han-tun (send forth their voice, or there is howling)

i-na-shi (means both it stopped, and it stood, or he stood up)

I-washi-CHU (loud white man's argument)

i-ya (the giant)

kok-tun toh-pa (four thousand)

Ko-la (my friend)

Ku-te I-yankapi (Shooting Chasing Him)

Lakotas (Sioux)

ma i-na-shi ye (Oh, look, it stood!)

Ma-sti- ja-la Wa-chipi (Dance of the rabbits)

mi-su (brother or cousin)

Ni tuka-shila mahiyaye he han-tan (Your grandfather went down to the west, or the sun went down)

og-leh-sha paha a-kan-ti heh (where Red Shirt lived on top of that table top)

pah-yahb-yah (in the middle ones)

Paha Sapa (Black Hills of South Dakota)

Paha he el ohk-la-te wi-cho-te ye-lo (Below the hill which we are facing is the camp)

Pan-keh-ska Wak-pa (North Platte River)

Pa-pa-sa-ka (dried up meat or jerky)

ptan-yetu (getting towards fall)

Suk-ma ni-tu (wild dog or timber wolf)

Ta-tanka kna-ski-yan (buffalo that become loco)

to-kas (enemies)

tun-hun (brother-in-law)

Tun-yun eh-he-lo (You have spoken indeed!)

Unkche kilah (fearless ones)

Wa-na-ki (Ghost)

Wanblee Wan-ka-te ya (High Eagle)

Wa-kan Tan-ka (Great Spirit)

Wak-pa Wash-teh (Good River)

wa-na-ki peh-shi (ghost weed)

Wa-na-ki Wi (Spirit woman)

wa-shi-i-ju (one who stole the tallow, or tallow stealer)

121

wa-shi-i-ju-wi-tko-tko kas (psychopathic tallow stealers)
wa-shi-i-ju-ki (tallow stealers or white men)
Wa-zi-ya taki-ya (Northwest)
Wi-yan or Wiyun (Woman)
Wo-pun (parfleche)
wo-yah-kehs-ah (Ones who cannot mind their lot)

Walking Bull's Tatanka Mani Camp 2005
By Diane Marie

Summer 2005 at Tatanka Mani Camp with Marilynn Bradley, Diane Marie, and Gilbert Walking Bull. Also pictured are Pispiza and Tashi.

Gilbert grew up on the Pine Ridge Reservation until he was in his late teens, when he moved off the reservation to make a life of his own. He began learning English as a range rider on a ranch in Wyoming, and from there traveled around to find his place in the white world. As a young man, he played semi-professional sports as a pitcher and first baseman for the Pittsburgh Pirates Farm Club. In 1965 he moved to Oregon where he settled down for twenty years and helped facilitate bringing back the native American Powwow to the Northwestern states. His vision has always been to help people reach the fullness of their lives. He believes that by teaching them the basic values and rituals he learned as a child, that all people will find peace and harmony within themselves and those around them. He believes that all people have a right to live to the fullness of their days, and that traditional Lakota principles are one way to live life as it was intended.

Gilbert and I met at the Wilderness Awareness School near Seattle, Washington, where we both lived and worked. With Gilbert's guidance I learned the sacred practice of running an Inipi, the sweat lodge. I ran a women's lodge for two years and began assisting him in sacred ceremony and in his teachings. We were married in 1999. In 2000 we decided to travel back to South Dakota to establish a center for the preservation of the basics of Lakota daily spiritual living through Lakota ceremony and song. We set out with our dear friend, Marilynn Bradley, to find a place for us to help Gilbert continue his work according to his vision. We were fortunate that first trip to find twenty-four acres in the lovely Southern Black Hills located just outside of Hot Springs, and Tatanka Mani Camp was born. Tatanka, in Lakota, means literally 'His greatest gift' and refers to the buffalo. Mani is translated as moving or walking. Together they mean walking buffalo. The name Tatanka Mani honors Gilbert as the spiritual leader, and also was chosen to represent something of the past moving into the future.

The first three years at Tatanka Mani were spent in cleaning up the land and remodeling the secondary structures to provide space for classes and living quarters for residents. We also began traveling whenever possible to help our extended family of friends across the country begin communities dedicated to Gilbert's vision. Now, as a result of the prayers and financial support of many wonderful people from all over the world, Tatanka Mani Camp is well established on twenty-four acres of gentle meadows and gentle hills of Ponderosa pines.

There are also five satellite communities around the country with solid desires to carry on the tradition as Gilbert has taught them. Even though I continue to assist Gilbert in the teachings and ceremonies provided through Tatanka Mani, both at home and across the country, I still consider myself a student of his. There is no end to the learning on this path.

We recently celebrated Gilbert's seventy-fifth birthday and we know we have been truly blessed in our lives. We will continue to provide all who pass this way a doorway into the Lakota traditions, as taught by someone who lived them, who continues to live them. Tatanka Mani is a spiritual center where people come to learn Lakota traditions and to participate in ceremonies. Lives are changed here and people are healed.

About a hundred people visit us in a typical year. Some stay for a class, some for a season. Our goal is to carry Gilbert's vision to all who are interested. In purchasing this book you have made a contribution to Tatanka Mani Camp and Gilbert's vision. We thank you.

To learn more about us, this camp, or our class schedule, please visit our web site: www.tatankamani.org.